MURDER IS
OUR MASCOT

a Schooled in Murder mystery

Tracy D. Comstock

This book is dedicated in loving memory to the woman who was always there for me and never stopped believing in me.

Without you, this book would not exist. You will always be one of the most vital parts of our hearts and souls. I love you, Gran. Forever.

Lois 'Colleen' Christopher
January 31, 1930-July 17, 2014

PROLOGUE

———

She had never thought about how dark and silent the hallways were without the rush of teenage bodies. Only the lights of the emergency exits at each end of the hallway gave out any illumination. She practically had to feel her way past the row of metal lockers to the stairwell. Turning left to take the stairs up to the teachers' lounge, she questioned yet again the urgency and necessity of this meeting. He had been adamant this discussion couldn't wait until tomorrow. Between the desperation in his voice and wanting what was sure to be a painful confrontation over with, she had reluctantly agreed. Hopefully, she would still be home in time to curl up with a cup of tea and her Yorkie pup, Duke, to catch the last hour of late-night *Golden Girls* reruns before turning in.

Turning instinctively to the right at the top of the stairs, she moved in the direction of the teachers' lounge, anxious to be done with this encounter. If only *the file* had not been mixed in with her guidance counseling files accidentally...but "if onlys" never got you anywhere. It would all be behind her soon anyway, one way or another.

As her hand closed over the doorknob to the teachers' lounge, she noticed a light under a door midway down the opposite side of the hall. That was odd, she thought. That light had to be coming from the copy room. Someone must have had to make some last-minute copies for classes tomorrow and forgotten to turn the light off. She was surprised, though, that the night custodians hadn't taken care of it. Perhaps it had just been overlooked. Oh well, it would only take her a second to turn it off. Always a practical woman, she saw no need to waste electricity. But when she pushed open the copy room door, it became suddenly, chillingly clear to her that electricity hadn't been the only thing wasted that evening. Her last thought, as the floor rushed up to meet her, was that Duke and the *Golden Girls* would have to wait after all.

CHAPTER ONE

———

The clack of Emily Taylor's high heels echoed hollowly in the deserted high school hallway. Normally, she loved the sound her heels made on the tile floor. Her obsession with high heels began when her height topped off at a gargantuan five feet and one inch, and their authoritative tapping sound typically made her feel confident and in charge. But not this morning. The click-clack reverberating off the rows of metal lockers seemed ominous, a warning of some kind.

Letting herself into her classroom, she decided that the school seemed somewhat sinister because she was unused to being there that early. Her great love affair with her snooze button meant that getting to school before it was filled with a mass of hormone-fueled teenagers was a rarity for her, but she had needed to get in early today in order to prep for a special before-school meeting with a student's mother. Stevie Davis was new to Ellington High and was really struggling in Emily's junior-level English class.

Something about Stevie tugged at Emily. He usually hid his eyes behind his fringe of bangs, causing Emily to fight the urge to grab her scissors and hack away at his curtain of hair so that she could see what was going on behind it. The few times he had tossed his hair back with the irritated shrug that was his typical answer to any question, his eyes had seemed sad, lost, or…something. Emily wasn't sure what that something was, but she was hoping that this meeting with his mother would shed some light on his issues.

Her cantankerous old computer whined to life as Emily flipped on her desk light. Dark, swollen clouds crowded the sky, swallowing her early morning classroom in shadows. Emily felt jumpy and spooked, as if those dark clouds were pressing down on her, enshrouding her in their gloom. Must be an allergy medicine-induced hangover making her feel strange this morning. Nothing like fall to get her sinuses going. As soon as she got her notes together for her meeting, she'd grab a cold shot of caffeine from the stash of sodas she kept in the teachers' lounge fridge. That would help clear her head. Or at least it would if Tad, the conference-hour-sharing, next-door math teacher and fellow soda junkie, hadn't depleted her supply.

As she pulled out samples of Stevie's writing and wrestled her computer into spitting out a copy of his grade report, the lights flickered. Glancing out the back wall of windows, Emily watched the increasing wind whip the trees into a frenzy. Multicolored fall leaves rained down like confetti. She usually loved the electric feel in the air before a good thunderstorm, but a loss of power would ruin her day's plans. Figuring she better make her copies before the ancient, temperamental copy machine went on the fritz, she began sorting through the piles on her desk for the paper she needed. They were organized piles, of course. Oh, who was she kidding? Trying to find the one thing she needed on her messy desk was like trying to isolate a single snowflake during a blizzard. Shuffling papers and files, Emily jumped at the first boom of thunder. The accompanying flash of lightning happened to spotlight the copy of the quiz for which she was searching. Hoping to entice Stevie into becoming more involved in class discussions, she was starting a unit on mythology since he had shown some interest in legends. Today's quiz was over the gods and goddesses of Mount Olympus, or it would be if she got her copies made in time.

Tucking all of her information for the meeting with Stevie's mother into a stray file folder, Emily grabbed up a fresh legal pad and pen and headed out the door. Halfway there, she turned on her heel to go back for the quiz she needed to copy. Yep, she definitely needed that soda. A glance at her vintage Strawberry Shortcake watch showed she was, as usual, cutting it close on time. But first things first.

Popping the top on the last soda in the fridge, Emily silently thanked whoever was the God of caffeine for their nectar as she took her first icy sip of the sugar-laden soda. No diet drinks for her, no sir, as the extra ten pounds on her hips could attest. Tad had tried to hide the last can behind a pitcher of green tea, knowing Emily would never touch that, even if it might benefit her hips. She, however, was on to his nefarious ways. Practicing her evil victory laugh, she click-clacked her way to the copy room to get her copies started before the meeting. Another crashing boom of thunder rattled the windows as Emily threw the door wide, propping it open with those cursed hips while she flipped the light switch. Nothing. Scanning the hallway confirmed her suspicions. The power was out. She took a step backward, thinking she would head downstairs to consult with Principal Matthews. Rain began to lash the windows over the stairwell, making the darkness of the hall seem even more complete. She fumbled her way a few feet down the hallway until the lights flickered back on again. Not wanting to waste a second in case the power decided to blink off again, Emily dashed back to the partially open copy room door. Hitting the light switch again with one hand, she rushed toward the hulking machine on the far wall. That was when papers went flying and sticky, syrupy soda sprayed everything in its path. Emily went airborne. Throwing her hands out in front of her to break her fall, Emily winced as they skidded through sticky wetness. The picture of grace she was not, so finding herself flat on her face was actually not uncommon for Emily. She could trip on a completely flat surface. The lights flickered again as she clambered to her feet, worrying about getting the sticky mess cleaned up before someone else slipped. Glancing down at her hands, she was busy cursing her lost lifeline, her last caffeine hit, when she realized that the sticky substance covering her hands was not soda. It was something thicker, and redder. Finally looking back to see what she had tripped over, Emily saw what appeared to be a head protruding from behind an office chair. Taking a cautious step closer, she could see that the head was surrounded by what looked like a puddle of congealing blood and was, thankfully, attached to a body. Unfortunately, it appeared to be a *dead* body. And that's when Emily began to scream and scream.

* * *

"I already told you once. I walked in and tripped over him." Emily couldn't seem to comprehend that she had stumbled over the lifeless body of Coach Layton, the head football coach who had regularly teased her about her clumsiness. She fought back tears and exhaustion as she went over the events of the morning for at least the fifth time with the police detective. She was huddled in the corner of the orange-and-brown flowered couch that took up one wall of the teacher's lounge. The couch was a relic, left behind from long-retired teachers, and still emitted the smell of stale cigarette smoke. Emily was sure it had seen its share of tears, and today her own soaked into the cushions to add to the collection. She hadn't moved from the couch since Mr. Matthews seated her still-hysterical self there after hearing her earlier screams and calling for help.

Mr. Matthews had put out a carefully worded notice that school was cancelled today due to "unforeseen circumstances." Emily had pulled herself together long enough to call Stevie's mother to cancel their meeting. She hadn't been sure what excuse she would give for the cancellation, but Arlene Davis had sounded oddly relieved not to have to meet with her and rushed off the phone, never asking for any explanation. Emily hadn't had much time to ponder the mother's strange reaction before the gangly-armed detective now sitting across from her, looking awkward with his long limbs scrunched into the hard plastic chair, had started questioning her.

The hallways certainly weren't deserted now. Emily didn't know, and wasn't sure she wanted to know, who all of the variously uniformed people were who were swarming throughout the school. Through the open door, she saw a gurney with a black body bag secured on it roll past. She quickly scrunched her eyes tightly closed, pretending that if she couldn't see it, it couldn't be real. With her eyes still shut, she slowly became aware that Detective Gangly-Arms was speaking to her.

"I know this must all have been a shock for you, ma'am, but I need to make sure I have these details down accurately." Gangly-Arms—no, wait—Welks, his name badge read, looked frazzled and exhausted, but Emily was in no mood to be placated.

"A shock? Yeah, I would say that's putting it mildly," Emily snapped.

This whole situation was surreal. Things like murder didn't happen here in Ellington, Missouri. This was a small, peaceful community. No, it was even more than that, Emily knew. This was her home, her town, the place where she had grown up and been happy to return to after several years of teaching in a much larger district up north. No, Emily was convinced that there had to be some mistake. This could not be happening. Not here, and not to her, a boring, law-abiding citizen whose only run-in with the police had been over her deplorable number of speeding tickets and her tendency to be slightly accident prone. To Emily, the roads were one big game of bumper cars. But murder? Uh-uh. Couldn't be happening.

"Detective, I just don't understand," Emily said.

"I know, Ms. Taylor," Detective Gangly-Arms slash Welks replied, almost apologetically.

Emily didn't recognize this detective so he must be relatively new to town, and she would bet her favorite collectable Smurfs lunchbox that this was his own first brush with murder. He looked about as green as she felt.

Glancing over her shoulder, she could still envision how Jim Layton had looked lying on the copy room floor less than an hour before. An hour? Could it really have been only an hour ago that she had been worrying about grading and lesson plans? She knew the sight of the football coach's lifeless body would haunt her in the days to come. She suppressed a shudder as she turned back to face the detective.

"It had to have happened after our night custodians left for the evening," Principal Matthews was saying to Detective Welks. Emily hadn't been aware Mr. Matthews had entered the room again, but she did notice that even he, a solid, sensible man who had spent the past twenty years at the helm of the school and witnessed a myriad of strange events, shied away from the word "murder." This was a novel concept for all of them.

"Otherwise, someone surely would have heard a struggle, don't you think?" Mr. Matthews continued, addressing both Emily and the detective.

"I do," Emily answered, nodding emphatically. "Jim Layton wasn't a quiet or passive man. If he had been arguing or struggling with someone, he definitely would have been overheard. Something like this couldn't have happened to Jim without him fighting back."

"I agree, Ms. Taylor." Detective Welks seemed to be debating on whether or not to say anything else. He must have decided there was no harm in Emily or Mr. Matthews knowing as he continued. "Mr. Layton had several lacerations on his hands and wrists. Looks like he probably died from blunt-force trauma to the back of his head, but it would appear that Mr. Layton did, in fact, struggle with his attacker."

Emily felt tears welling up again. What a tragic waste of life. Who would have wanted to hurt Jim? Granted, Emily hadn't known Jim Layton that well on a personal level, but he had never struck her as an especially violent or despicable man. He had appeared to be what he was—the typical football coach focused on obtaining a winning season. But unlike other coaches Emily had worked with, Jim never acted like he was above the rules followed by the rest of the teaching staff. He had seemed to genuinely care about not only the athletic but the academic success of his players as well. Emily had admired the interest Jim took in his athletes. His players and their parents seemed to respect him, and he was the guy who was always ready with a joke, making everyone laugh at faculty meetings and such. Emily couldn't fathom what reason anyone could possibly have to hate Jim Layton enough to end his life this way.

Emily tuned back in to hear Mr. Matthews saying, "Emily? You look like you're about ready to drop. Why don't you go on home and get some rest? It's okay for her to leave now, isn't it, Detective?"

"Of course. We have all the information we need from Ms. Taylor for now. If you would, though, come by the station and sign your statement later this afternoon, okay?"

"Yes, I will," Emily mumbled, then headed for her classroom to retrieve her things, grateful to be leaving the gruesome events of the morning behind her, if only for a little while.

CHAPTER TWO

———

"Ick!" Goose bumps pebbled Emily's flesh as she peeled out of the red turtleneck and wide-legged black pants she had worn to school that day. She stuffed them into a large black trash bag she had hauled into the bathroom. Steam billowed out of the waiting shower. As soon as she took a turn under the scalding water, she planned to throw the entire outfit in the dumpster, even if she had picked up her shoes on sale at Macy's only the week before. Said red patent leather pumps had been left by the door, since she didn't want to risk tracking sticky soda and goodness knows what else across her floors. Now that she was home and surrounded by her own familiar and comforting things, she was anxious to divest herself of any remains of this awful day.

Twenty minutes later, feeling somewhat better after scrubbing herself raw, she shrugged into a pair of well-worn jeans and an Ellington High sweatshirt. She ran a brush through her still-wet chestnut bob, then headed to the kitchen in search of another soda. Hey, no judging. It had been a long morning and, in her defense, she *had* spilled her first one of the day.

Staring out the small window over her sink, she noticed that the storm showed no signs of abating. Emily switched on a few lamps to push back the gloom as she headed to her bedroom for a pair of warm socks. She was tugging on her shoes, preparing to make a mad dash to the dumpster, when she heard a sharp yip. It had to be Duke, Helen's dog, barking next door. Helen Burning, the high school counselor and Emily's neighbor in the duplex next door, had become fast friends with Emily's mom when they had bonded at a pottery-making class. Emily's mom was notorious for exploring new creative outlets.

Emily had found out the hard way that she was allergic to Duke when she had offered to "dog sit" him one weekend while Helen went to visit some friends in the city. Since then, she had kept her distance, but she rarely heard a peep out of him. He was a well-behaved dog. Emily wondered what was bothering him. Maybe he was glad to have Helen home early. Emily hadn't seen Helen at the school this morning, but maybe they had missed each other amid all the confusion. Emily wanted to offer her services in any way she could, knowing the students would be upset and confused when they heard the news of the coach's death. Especially Stevie. Jim had been the one person who had been able to forge a connection with the withdrawn new student. She would give Helen a call later, she thought as she sprinted through the pelting rain, slamming the dumpster lid on her discarded clothes.

She had just regained her porch when her mother's car pulled into her drive. Emily left the door open and toed off her sopping shoes. Her mom hurried in the door right behind her, shutting out the wind and rain. Knowing this was bound to be a trying conversation, Emily grabbed up her soda can from where she had left it on the coffee table. Her mom hung up her raincoat on one of the hooks by the door and turned to frown at the open soda in Emily's hand. "Don't start," Emily warned, motioning her to follow into the kitchen. She stuck a mug of water to heat in the microwave for her mom's preferred herbal tea. Emily shuddered at the smell alone, wondering how she could come from someone who would drink such a vile substance.

Surprised by her mom's silence, Emily started the conversation. "How did you find out? Did Helen call you?" Turning to hand her mom her tea, she finally took in her mom's appearance. She had on a pair of loudly striped orange-and-hot-pink capri pants, paired with a turquoise cable-knit sweater and the most hideous pair of dark green mud boots Emily had ever seen.

"What in the world are you wearing?" Emily asked before her mom could answer her.

"Oh," Emily's mom, the impetuous Susan Taylor, glanced down at herself and waved her hand dismissively. "All I could think of after hearing the news was getting over here to you. I grabbed the first things that came to hand." Emily silently decided it was time to help her mom weed through her closet if these were the first things that came to hand.

Out loud she said, "Thanks for coming, Mom."

Emily relived all of the details of the awful morning with her mom but didn't feel any better for having shared the story. Instead she felt angry and helpless. Angry at whoever had committed such a violent act and helpless to do anything to change things. Both she and her mom watched the lightning play across the sky through the window over Emily's breakfast nook. They were uncharacteristically silent. Emily assumed they were both thinking how futile words were in this situation—they could change nothing.

Emily was the first to break the silence by asking, "So, when did Helen call you?"

"Oh, Helen didn't. Tad called your father." Emily should have guessed. Tad Higginbotham, or Theodore, as Emily's dad called him, had been one of her dad's favorite students when he taught history at Ellington High. He and her dad had remained in touch over the years, and now Tad was her soda-stealing neighbor from the class next door. A flash of lightning lit up the kitchen as Emily started to make a comment about Tad being a tattletale. But her words were swallowed up by a deafening crack of thunder. Darkness followed as the power once again went out. Emily headed to her utility drawer for a flashlight, but her mom had already whipped out a lighter and lit the candle Emily kept in the center of her table. Emily stared at her mom in surprise as the homey scents of vanilla and cinnamon filled the room.

Emily asked, "Really, Mom? What the heck are you doing with a lighter?" Her mom had given up smoking before Emily was even born.

"Um…for incense," was Susan's mysterious reply. "Look, I gotta head out. Call me later." And then she dashed out the door before Emily could even form a response.

* * *

Emily watched her mom's headlights slice through the downpour, then turned to survey her darkened living room.

Emily lit a few more candles and decided now was as good a time as any to get caught up on some grading. After her second essay on the themes in *Macbeth*, she felt herself slipping into a grading coma. By the sixth essay, she was drooling. She dreamed of Lady Macbeth's blood-stained hands and Jim's lifeless body. When a sound awoke her, she was both relieved and disoriented. Springing off the couch, she sent papers cascading to the floor. Her heart was pounding. What had she heard? A piercing bark sounded. Duke. That was the sound that had woken her. This was definitely not normal behavior for him. Maybe she should make sure things were okay. She needed to talk to Helen anyway.

A quick glance out the front window showed that the rain still had not let up, so she grabbed a raincoat before making the quick dash between her duplex's front porch and Helen's. She pounded on Helen's front door and shivered, waiting for Helen to answer. By the time her teeth were chattering and she had pounded her fist sore, Helen still hadn't come to the door. Maybe she hadn't made it home yet? Squishing through puddles, Emily made her way around Helen's side of the duplex to look in the kitchen windows. Duke was pacing and clawing at the door. The poor guy looked desperate to go out, but there was no sign of Helen, and her trusty Tahoe wasn't in the carport either. Figuring this was as close to an emergency as she needed to use the spare key Helen had given her a while back, Emily rushed back to her own duplex, grabbing the key off a hook by the door. She had barely gotten Helen's door open, when Duke raced out between her legs to cower under the front maple to do his business. Emily grabbed a towel out of the linen closet and met Duke at the door, wiping down his paws. She followed him as he padded back into the kitchen toward his food and water bowls. His empty and dry food and water bowls. What the heck? Helen might not have made it home yet this morning, but she wouldn't have left Duke without fresh food and water.

A quick glance in the bedroom showed the bed still neatly made. That wasn't really surprising, though. Helen was a neat freak. There were no breakfast dishes in the sink either, so could that mean Helen hadn't been home last night? Or had she just straightened everything up before leaving for school this morning? While a foreign concept to Emily, she knew that some people actually preferred things neat and tidy, not chaotic and "piled." Emily turned a circle in the empty kitchen. Duke whined, so she went ahead and refilled his food and water bowls, which he attacked like a tiny, ravenous wolf.

Helen had been at school yesterday— Emily had talked to her on her way out. So did she ever come home? Emily had been in her allergy medicine-induced coma before dark, so she wouldn't have heard anything from next door even if Helen had been holding a rave. Which, of course, was highly unlikely. So if Helen hadn't come home last night, then where was she now? And did she even know about Jim Layton's murder?

Leaving Duke happily munching away, Emily used Helen's landline to call Tad. His phone rang several times before he answered with a wary, "Hello? Tad Higginbotham."

"It's me, Emily. I'm calling from Helen's duplex."

"That would explain why I didn't recognize the number. A landline? Really? I wasn't sure anyone had those anymore, though they definitely come in handy in weather like this."

Emily rolled her eyes. Why did every conversation with Tad sound like a lecture? "Listen, I don't have time to debate the merits of landlines with you right now. Have you seen Helen?"

"Are you okay, Pitbull?" Tad had called her Pitbull ever since they were teens. He always said she was like an attack dog if she didn't get her way or she was defending someone she loved—she'd bite your leg off and then beat you with it. Emily hated the nickname, which was probably why Tad insisted on continually using it.

"What? No, I'm fine. I just want to know if you've seen Helen since school yesterday."

"You told me that you're calling from Helen's place. Aren't you looking at her? Are you in trouble? What's going on?"

"Whoa there, Cowboy. I'm fine. Duke was barking his head off, so I came to check things out. When he clearly needed to uh…use the facilities, I used the spare key Helen gave me to let him out. His food and water bowls are both empty. Did you go up to the school today? Did you see Helen there?"

Finally full, Duke came over and stared up at Emily with sad, brown eyes. He put his paws on her leg, begging for attention. She wished she could give his belly a good rub, but she knew if she touched him, she would be toast. Her allergies were already in full swing, and one touch of that dog, and she would be one giant snot ball.

"No, Pit. I haven't seen Helen since I left school yesterday. I did go up to school this morning. I always try to get there early, as you know, to be fully prepared for the day." Emily gave another eye roll. "But instead, I found the place crawling with cops. I talked to Principal Matthews, and he told me what happened. I'm really sorry you had to be the one to find him, Em." Tad's voice lowered in sympathy. Emily tried to smother the fluttery feeling in the pit of her stomach at his warm, caring voice.

Instead, she paused to clear her throat. "What should I do about Duke?" Ears perking up at the mention of his name, Duke lay down at Emily's feet, baring his little, pink belly. "He needs looking after, and I'm allergic."

Tad laughed deeply. "I'd forgotten that. Ironic. The Pitbull is allergic to the Yorkie." This time Emily not only rolled her eyes, she also snarled. Tad hastily continued, "I can take him. The Cruises won't mind if he stays here temporarily." Tad lived in a converted loft above the local hardware store. The Cruise family had run the store for years. Emily had fond memories of that loft space, but not because Tad lived there. The summer before her freshman year of high school, she and the Cruises' youngest son, Josh, had snuck up to what was then an empty loft to share their first kiss.

"Great. I'll gather up his supplies and bring him to you." It was only after she hung up that Emily realized she should have had Tad come to them. There was no way she could transport Duke without touching him. Oh well, sacrifices, sacrifices.

* * *

Drenched and out of breath, Emily banged on Tad's door. He opened it, looking both amused and sexy, which only irritated Emily more. She thrust dog accoutrements at him, blowing hair out of her eyes. Tad scooped up the dog carrier at the top of the stairs, leading the way into his apartment. "How did you get Duke in here if you can't touch him without sneezing your head off?" he asked. He let Duke out and the dog sniffed around and then settled comfortably on the bed Tad had made for him in the living room. Tad and Duke were apparently old friends.

Emily, trying not to feel left out by their instant male bonding, huffed, "Lucky for me, Helen had a pair of rubber gloves under the sink. Unlucky for Helen, she now needs a new pair." Tad snorted out a laugh, which he adroitly turned into a cough.

"So, what should we do now?" Emily asked. Now that Duke was safely delivered and she had caught her breath, she took a good look around her. Her eyes widened at the large number of candles bathing Tad's apartment in a warm glow due to the power outage. The apartment suddenly felt too small to contain the both of them. She felt her cheeks warm and quickly backtracked to rephrase her earlier question. "I mean, what should we do about Helen?"

Tad watched Emily silently for a few seconds. A few very long seconds, she thought. Tad had shown her absolutely no attention in high school, unless you counted his smirks and nicknames. Emily had had a huge crush on him as a freshman, but he had seemed oblivious to her very presence. Once he graduated, Emily had moved on, developing many more crushes over the years. But once both she and Tad had returned to town and they had ended up teaching together, Emily noticed that Tad no longer ignored her. In fact, there were times when she thought there might even be something brewing.

Tad finally broke eye contact and said, "Well, Nancy, I think we'd better head up to the school and see what we can find out. Duke seems to be fine." They both looked over to where Duke was sound asleep, snuffling out little dog snores.

"Alrighty, then, let's go. But 'Nancy?'" Emily questioned.

"Nancy Drew. I bet you read every one you could get your hands on when you were growing up, right?" And there was the smirk again.

"No comment." Emily tossed her head and headed out the door, leaving Tad to follow.

CHAPTER THREE

———

Tad insisted on their taking his sensible black Prius, refusing to set foot in what he called "Emily's deathtrap." Emily had bought her red PT Cruiser when she graduated from college. It had been all shiny and new then, but even Emily couldn't deny that it had seen better days. Besides her penchant for speeding, she also tended to multitask when she drove. Apparently reading and driving was *not* considered a way to better utilize time to most people. But despite its dents and dings, Emily knew it would be a long time before she could bear to part with her beloved car. She thought her PT looked very British. It's what she imagined Hercule Poirot would drive if Agatha Christie were still alive to create more mysteries for him and his little "gray cells" to solve. Clearly, Emily was a true Anglophile. Her dream was to visit London one day, but so far, the closest she had come was pinning sites to visit on her Places to Go Pinterest board.

Emily wiggled in her seat. She felt like they were traveling at the speed of snail. "Can't you go any faster, Grandpa?"

Tad merely glanced her way, never taking his hands off their ten and two position. "No. That's why my car doesn't look like it's been through a demolition derby."

Emily resisted, barely, the temptation to stick her tongue out at him. She wracked her mind for a witty comeback, but Tad's subtle cologne was penetrating her brain, clouding her senses. She settled for giving him the cold shoulder, staring out the passenger-side window instead. The rain was still coming down. An occasional rumble of thunder shook the heavens. Suddenly, Emily became aware of what she was actually staring at.

She smacked Tad's shoulder. "Look! The power must be back on." Lights were blooming in the windows of the houses they passed on their way to the school. The school itself, however, looked fairly deserted. The light was on in Principal Matthews's office and in a classroom at the far end of the second floor. Two vehicles were in the employee parking lot when they pulled in. One was Principal Matthews's black Ford 4x4. The other vehicle looked brand new, its temporary plate stuck in the back window.

Emily could have sworn Tad had to swipe at a drop of drool as he took in the sleek, forest-green Cobra parked beside them.

"Who in the heck drives that?" Emily asked.

Tad's only response was a shrug as he was still too busy checking out the car. "One lucky guy," he finally muttered.

"Or gal," Emily corrected before she hurried through the steadily falling rain to the main doors.

Inside, Emily stopped to shake rain off like a wet dog. Tad rushed in behind her, running a hand through his own sopping hair and scattering droplets of water. Still dripping, they headed toward Principal Matthews's office. Rounding the long counter that separated his office from the secretary's work area, Emily tugged at Tad's shirt, pulling him back so she could whisper to him.

"What?" Tad snapped in a hoarse whisper.

"Look at him. I almost hate to bother him. Have you ever seen him look so…well, not like himself?"

Tad peeked over her shoulder and nodded. "Yeah, he looks like a drowning man. A murder in his school has to be devastating for him. Wish I had a lifeline to throw him. At least we can show him some support."

Emily still hesitated before she knocked on his door. Principal Matthews always wore a tie, even to sporting events. He was fastidious about how he ran his school and was the same about his appearance. Everything about him always exuded confidence and professionalism. But right now, he was slumped at his desk, his head in his hands. His tie had been jerked askew and the top few buttons of his shirt were undone. His thick gray mane was disheveled. Emily was engulfed in waves of guilt, although she knew it wasn't exactly her fault that she had stumbled over a dead body in the school. But still, she hated to add to his concern. Maybe they should wait until later to talk to him about Helen and her possible disappearance.

Tad, apparently, had no such qualms. He strode through the door and clapped a hand on Principal Matthews's shoulder. The older man looked up, startled, but then seeing who was in his office, he gave them a small smile. Emily eased into one of the chairs in front of his massive desk. She squirmed uncomfortably. She knew she was being ridiculous, but she still felt like a student about to be chastised, nevertheless.

"How are things going?" Tad asked, taking the chair next to Emily's. She noticed he appeared totally at ease. He'd probably never seen the inside of the principal's office in high school, Emily thought, unless it was to receive some kind of merit award. She inched away from Mr. Perfect. Tad shot her a quizzical glance, but Emily focused on Principal Matthews.

"The police are through upstairs. They're sending over some people they know to clean so we can have the school up and running again tomorrow. I can't believe we've had this, this—atrocity happen here. Emily, are you okay?"

Principal Matthews's eyes were full of genuine concern, and Emily had to fight to speak over the sudden lump in her throat.

"I'm fine. Really," she reiterated when he lowered his brows at her. "I'm sorry about everything. And I certainly don't want to add to your worries, but have you seen Helen recently?"

"Helen? No, actually, I haven't. I checked her office earlier to see about coordinating some grief counseling for the students, but she wasn't there. I've left a message on her voice mail. Why do you ask? Is something wrong?" He looked like a man on a ledge. Emily didn't want to be the one who made him leap.

"I'm sure it's nothing," Tad was quick to reassure him. "Emily heard Duke barking and let him out to do his business. She saw that his food and water bowls were empty, and we all know Helen loves that dog like her own child, but I'm sure she just got caught up somewhere due to the weather. Now that the power is back on, she's sure to turn up soon."

"Okay. If you say so. That doesn't sound like Helen, though. I'll try to call her again later. If you hear anything, let me know, and I'll do the same."

"Of course. Anything else we can do?" Emily asked.

"No, I think I've got it under control."

As they stood up to leave, Tad stopped to ask Principal Matthews about the Cobra in the parking lot.

"Oh, that's Mr. Barnes's. I think he purchased it recently. He's been a big help to me today. I didn't realize he was still here, though. Must be working on lesson plans." Principal Matthews looked down at the notes on his desk, and Emily and Tad took that as their cue to leave.

Once they were back out in the hallway, Tad headed to the main doors, but Emily turned to the stairs. "Where are you going?"

Tad looked exasperated, but Emily gave him a grim smile. "To find out why Mr. Barnes has been here all day, that's where." She continued up the stairs and was not surprised to hear Tad following her. She was grateful for his presence when she reached the second floor. She didn't want to look in the direction of the copy room, but her eyes had other ideas. As if drawn by a magnet, her head swiveled in that direction. Yellow crime scene tape still sealed off the room, denying anyone access. Emily felt sick to her stomach when she thought of what the cleaning crew would have to deal with. She shuddered, feeling a bit faint. Tad placed his hand on the small of her back, urging her toward the other end of the hall. She knew he was trying to comfort her, and while she appreciated his efforts, it would be some time before she would feel comfortable going anywhere near that copy room.

A light shone under Mr. Barnes's door. Emily had never particularly liked Mr. Barnes. He was one of those obnoxious know-it-alls. He rubbed everyone the wrong way, maybe due to his penchant for correcting people on any and every thing, every chance he got. Especially in front of a crowd. This definitely made for some fun faculty meetings. Jim had been the one who could lighten the mood with a joke or two when Mr. Barnes was on a roll. Everyone knew that Mr. Barnes was not a fan of Coach Layton. Jim hadn't seemed to care one way or the other, and Emily had admired that about him. As for Mr. Barnes, she had yet to find anything to admire, and she *had* looked. She had been taught to always look for the best in people. But Mr. Barnes was a black hole, devoid of positive qualities. He definitely knew his stuff chemistry-wise, but his personality was off-putting to students too. They took his classes only because they had to.

Emily and Tad could see through the small window in his door that Mr. Barnes was working at his computer, his back to them. Tad was going to knock, but Emily turned the doorknob instead. She was surprised to find it locked.

Mr. Barnes started and turned to glare at them when he heard them rattling his door. He stomped over and pulled the door open a crack. "What do you two want?"

"Nice to see you too, Mr. Barnes," Emily said pleasantly as she forced her way past him, Tad on her heels. "You've certainly been working hard today, haven't you? Principal Matthews said you've been here all day."

"Is there a crime against wanting to be prepared, Ms. Taylor? Some of us don't wait until the last minute to get our things organized for class." He pointedly stared at Emily. She could feel her cheeks getting warm and figured they now looked like a baby's butt with a severe diaper rash, but, man, did this guy know how to push her buttons or what? She started to tell him exactly what she thought of his "preparedness" but felt Tad's hand on her back again. This time the gesture was not meant for comfort but as a warning. She silently fumed while Mr. Barnes watched her with his cold, beady eyes. He reminded her of a rat. A big rat. A big, ugly rat. A big, ugly rat that she would like to catch in a trap. Then she would…

Tad interrupted her silent tirade against Mr. Barnes, and their staring contest, by pointing to the windows and asking, "Hey, Richard, Principal Matthews said the Cobra out in the parking lot is yours. When did you get her? She sure is a beauty." He and Barnes headed toward the windows to check out the "beauty." Emily didn't bother to move. "Why are cars always referred to by feminine pronouns?" she asked instead.

"You're the English teacher—you tell us," was Barnes's reply.

Emily fought an internal battle between walking out the door or beaning Barnes with one of his own textbooks. She settled for the former, making her way down to her own room. That jerk was right about one thing, she fumed, unlocking her own door and flipping on the lights. She did need to prepare for tomorrow. She still hadn't made copies of that quiz, but the thought of going near the copy room caused her to feel faint again. She fell into her desk chair, sticking her head between her knees, deciding she would run the copies off on her own printer instead. What was the cost of a little paper and ink as opposed to her health and well-being, right?

A few minutes later, Tad found her still sitting with her head between her legs. "How's the view down there?"

Emily flipped her head back up and then wished she hadn't as the room spun from the head rush. "I've never noticed before how intricate the tile work is on our floors. You should check it out sometime. When you're not bonding over your lust for sports cars with Richard Barnes, that is."

Tad pulled up a student desk, planting his rear on the top of it and his feet in the seat. "Well, if you hadn't run out so fast, you could have heard the interesting gossip Richard had to share."

"I would never let my students sit in their desks that way. Off." Emily snapped her fingers at Tad like he was an unruly student. "But I'll let it go—for now—if you'll tell me what you found out."

"Gee, thanks, Teach. OCD much?" Tad leaned against the wall instead, watching her meticulously align the desk back in its proper row. Emily simply ignored him. "Okay, here's the deal," Tad continued. "A couple of days ago, as Richard was heading out for the day, he overheard two people arguing in Helen's office. "

"And naturally, being him, he eavesdropped…" The slimy, sneaking rat, she added in her head.

"Right. So he says Helen was arguing with Coach Layton. He never really heard what they were arguing about, but he says he heard something about going to the police with the information."

Tad crossed his arms, looking very proud of himself. Emily stared right through him, thinking about what Barnes had overheard. "What information? Which one wanted to go to the police?" she asked.

Tad's face fell. "I don't know. I didn't ask about that part. But he did say that he hasn't seen Helen today and that he's already told the police about the argument he overhead."

At the mention of the police, Emily hopped up like a jack-in-the-box. "That reminds me. I was supposed to stop by the station and sign my statement this afternoon." She made a beeline for the door.

"Your carriage awaits, madam," Tad quipped as he followed her out, turning the lights off behind them.

* * *

Emily chewed her thumbnail as Tad drove through the gathering darkness. The rain was finally letting up, but the day was drawing to a close. Emily was silent as Tad pulled up in front of the brick building which housed Ellington's finest.

Tad tapped her shoulder, forcing her to face him. "Want me to go in with you?" Emily nodded. She hadn't wanted Tad to know how nervous she was. It wasn't that she was guilty of anything, unless sarcasm was a crime. It was that being here, signing a statement, reminded her of finding Jim all over again. And to top off her worry tank, there was Helen's disappearance. "Should we say anything about not being able to locate Helen?" Emily asked Tad as they headed toward the glass double doors.

Tad motioned for her to go ahead. "I think we'd better say as little as possible. We don't want to cast unfair aspersions." Only Tad could get away with using such a hoity-toity word as "aspersions."

"What?" he asked. Emily ignored him, going up to the front counter to announce herself. Detective Gangly-Arms himself came out of a back room as Emily was reviewing her statement.

"Anything you want to add? Anything else you remember?" he asked her.

She shook her head regretfully. The thought of Helen missing ping-ponged around in her brain, but she ignored it. Instead she blurted out, "We did just have a conversation with

Richard Barnes up at the school, though. Did you happen to see that brand-new Cobra he's driving? I can't help wondering how he came up with the money to buy that. I mean, I'm a teacher too, and I sure couldn't afford that kind of car, know what I mean?"

Tad was staring at her open-mouthed and Detective Gangly-Arms glowered at her from under lowered eyebrows. "What exactly are you trying to say, Ms. Taylor? Is there a reason that we should be looking closer at Richard Barnes? If you know something, you better tell me."

Emily blushed. No, she didn't have any hard evidence, but if being a smarmy, repulsive rodent wasn't reason enough, well…what could she say?

"We'll be going now. Thank you for your time, Detective." Tad took her by the elbow and guided her none too gently out the doors. Once they were out of hearing, Emily shook free of his viselike grip. "What was that about?" he asked her. "You made Richard sound like some kind of criminal."

"For all we know, he is. He's the most loathsome creature I've ever met. Aren't you the teensiest bit curious as to how he can afford that kind of car on the salary we make?"

Tad didn't answer her. He moved around to the driver's side of the car and got in. Emily had no choice but to follow suit. "Well?" she prompted once she was buckled in.

Tad waited until they were underway to answer. "I guess I am a little curious. But you had no reason to make him sound guilty of something. Is this because you're worried Helen is involved somehow?"

"No!" Emily pushed at her hair, shrugging at the confines of her seat belt. "Okay, maybe a little. What other explanation do we have?" Emily flounced back in her seat, stung by the fact that maybe Tad was right. Darn it all, the truth really did hurt, didn't it? She might have been a smidge out of line, but Barnes was, and always would be, a snake in her book. Maybe he hadn't killed Jim, but she'd wager her second-best Care Bears lunchbox that he was guilty of some kind of crime, even if it was just being a nasty human being.

Emily was still pouting at being called out when they pulled up in front of Cruise's Hardware. "Listen, Em," Tad started, trying to smooth things over, "I know how worried you are about Helen. I am too. You've been through a lot today. Why don't you go home and try to get some rest?" Emily realized she was bone-weary, but the thought of going back to her empty duplex didn't sound too appealing. For Tad's sake, she nodded and trudged toward her own car.

"Good luck with Duke," she called back over her shoulder before driving away. She had gone less than a block when her phone started blaring out Ozzy Osbourne's "Crazy Train." Emily scooped it up from the center console, seeing from the caller ID display that it was Gabby.

"Hey," she answered.

"Hey, back. You sound wiped. Some day, huh?" She and Gabriella "Gabby" Spencer had been best friends since kindergarten when Emily had punched Buddy Lines in the nose for trying to kiss Gabby on the playground. They had had each other's backs ever since.

"Yeah, some day." Emily's weariness was growing by the second.

"You sound tired, so you might not be interested, but I was calling to invite you over for dinner in case you didn't want to be alone." The invitation perked Emily up. After graduation, while Emily had headed off to college to pursue her dream of becoming a teacher, Gabby had married her high school sweetheart, Greg Spencer, and settled comfortably into the role of wife and mother. Emily was godmother to their adorable twin girls, Abigail and Phoebe, who were now two-year-old bundles of joy, or terror, depending on the day. Being surrounded by Gabby's crazy, loud, loving family sounded much better than spending the night alone.

"What can I bring?"

"Just yourself. See you around 7:00." Seeing she still had an hour, Emily decided to swing by home to see if Helen had surfaced. She was disappointed to see both sides of the duplex dark as she pulled up. To be sure, she walked around to check Helen's carport. Nope, still empty. Maybe her mom had heard something.

Emily let herself in her front door and locked it securely behind her. Even though her duplex was as cozy and warm as usual, she shivered. She couldn't get past the idea that there was a murderer out there somewhere and wondered if she would ever truly feel safe again. Trying to stave off the unsettling feeling, Emily switched on a few lights and headed into the kitchen for her own form of fortification. Yep, caffeine. She settled into her breakfast nook, admiring her row of vintage lunchboxes parading around the top of the kitchen cabinets. Although she had barely been born in the '80s, she loved everything about the decade. Every one of her lunchboxes on display hearkened back to the era of big hair, neon colors, and parachute pants. Okay, maybe she didn't love the fashion sense of the '80s, but she definitely loved the cartoons. Smiling back at a friendly My Little Pony, she dialed her mom.

She answered on the first ring. "How're you doing, Em? Is everything okay? Any news? Do you want to come over for supper?"

"Okay. I guess so. Not that I've been told. And thanks, but Gabby invited me to eat at her house." Talking with her mom should be an Olympic sport, she decided. How many questions can someone ask you before you can no longer remember and answer them in the correct order? "Actually, Mom, the reason I was calling was to see if you had heard from Helen today."

"Helen? No. I haven't heard a word from her since our landscape painting class Tuesday evening. Isn't she home?"

Emily explained about Duke and how no one had seen Helen since the end of the school day yesterday. Her mom was quiet for so long, Emily finally prompted "Mom?" to the silent line.

"I'm worried, Em. Helen would never leave Duke without food or water like that. Something has to be wrong. Should we call the police and file a missing person's report?"

Emily hesitated. Would pointing out Helen's absence to the police cast suspicion on her? "I'm not sure, Mom. Surely she'll turn up soon." Emily didn't want to upset her mom further by mentioning the argument Barnes had supposedly overheard between Helen and Jim. Emily didn't think they should put much stock in anything the slimeball had to say, anyway.

"Call me the minute you hear something. And give those girls of Gabby's a kiss for me." Emily assured her mom she would. Checking the clock, she realized that time had, as usual, gotten away from her. She scurried around, changing clothes, running a brush through her hair, and at the last minute, going back to leave a few lights burning so she didn't have to come home to a dark house. *I'm like the White Rabbit in* Alice in Wonderland, Emily thought as she pulled out of her drive. *I'm always late, late for a very important date.* Wishing she had fallen through the looking glass and this whole day would turn out to be a dream, Emily headed toward Gabby's big, farm-style home on the edge of town.

* * *

Welcoming lights glowed in the large picture windows framing the front of the house. Walking up the sidewalk, Emily could see Abigail and Phoebe playing what looked to be a game of tea party. She could hear them giggling and Gabby singing in the kitchen. Emily felt a stab of longing. Yes, she was happy with her life, but at times like this, she envied Gabby her perfect little family. Still, she knew by the time she left, a dose of the twin tornadoes would leave her thankful for the peace and quiet of her own small abode. Inhaling a bracing breath of the cold, damp air, she pushed her way through the door and into the warmth, craziness, and cacophony. Dexter, the Spencers' spoiled dalbrador, came nosing up for a scratch, sniffing to see if she came bearing food. Disappointed when he didn't find any, he ambled away, only to be replaced by two monkeys crawling all over Emily, pulling at her pockets, and sticking a tiara on her head.

"Tea party! Princess!" Phoebe chirped.

"You be princess. We princesses. Right, Mommy?" Abigail chimed in. Gabby reached down to help Emily off with her coat as the girls had already pulled her to the floor to join them. She gave Emily a *what can you do* shrug and sat down too.

Abigail, her dark curls swinging, played the part of hostess until she tired of the game and ran off to play with the pile of denuded Barbies in the girls' play alcove. Phoebe hugged Emily tightly before scurrying off to join her sister.

"Spill." Gabby was perched on the edge of her seat, eager to hear the latest news.

"Well, first of all…" Emily trailed off as her phone began to ring, the sound muffled by her purse. "Sorry, Gabby, but I'd better check this. It's been a weird day." She finally managed to free her phone from the clinging receipts and debris covering the depths of her purse and checked to see who was calling. She stabbed the answer button. "What's wrong, Mom?" she asked without preamble.

"I'm sorry to bother you while you're at Gabby's, but I wanted you to know that I went ahead and called the police station." Of course you did, Emily thought. Out loud, she said, "What'd you find out?"

"Nothing! That Detective Welks," Gangly-Arms, Emily silently amended, "told me that Helen hasn't been missing long enough to file a missing person's report. I had the distinct impression that he was trying to get me off the phone. He wasn't listening to me at all!"

Her mom was on the verge of tears, and Emily wasn't sure what to say or do. Finally she settled on, "How about we give it until tomorrow morning? If Helen's still not back by then, I'll go down to the station with you to file a formal report."

This seemed to mollify her mom a little. She was still sniffling but seemed calmer as they said their good-byes and hung up. Gabby immediately pounced, "What was that all about? Where's Helen? How does this relate to Jim Layton's death?"

Emily took a gulp of wine from the glass Gabby handed her. "Gabby, you sound like Mom right now."

Gabby had the good grace to look embarrassed. She settled back into her comfy chair. "Sorry, when you're ready to talk, I'm ready to listen."

Emily went through the entire story, including finding Duke and the trip she and Tad had made to the school and the police station. "So, I think Barnes is involved somehow. I don't know where Helen is, but I know she's no killer," she finally concluded.

Gabby shook back her hair and checked to see that the twins were still playing peacefully. "I don't know, Em. I feel like you're telling me the plot of a mystery novel you just read. All of this"—she waved her hands over her head as if encompassing the whole ordeal—"seems unbelievable. This is Ellington, for goodness' sake. Nothing exciting ever happens here, unless you count Old Man Fillmore streaking through the town square after he'd had too much to drink last New Year's Eve."

Emily choked on a sip of wine as she laughed at the memory. Watching the twins play with their naked dolls, Emily noticed how content and happy their little faces looked. For some reason, that thought brought Stevie to mind. Stevie looked lost, Emily thought, not content, not happy. She was explaining to Gabby about Stevie and why she was concerned when Greg walked in the back door. He immediately crossed to Gabby to plant a kiss on her forehead. As he hung up his coat, Emily pouted. "Where's my kiss?" Greg dutifully crossed to where she was sitting and plastered a sloppy, Saint Bernard-like kiss on her forehead too.

"Watch it, Emily. That's my man you're flirting with there," Gabby joked. "For that, you get to help me finish supper."

The adults all trooped to the kitchen. While Emily set the table, Greg filled glasses and sippy cups. "Were you talking about Stevie Davis by any chance?" he asked Emily.

Emily turned to him in surprise, dropping one of the forks she was placing on the table. "Yeah. He's in my junior-level English class, and he's really struggling. He was close with Coach Layton. I'm worried how Jim's death may affect him. I was supposed to meet with his mom this morning, but with, well, you know"—Emily stopped to gulp in air—"I had to cancel."

Greg patted her shoulder. "Hang in there, kid. You're tougher than you think you are."

Emily gave him a weak smile. "How do you know him?" she asked.

"I've worked with his mom, Arlene, on several real estate deals."

"Of course." Emily smacked her forehead. "I had forgotten that she was in the real estate business. I need to call her first thing tomorrow and get that meeting rescheduled. I know he's capable of doing the work. I just have to figure out what his deal is."

"I'm sure his mom will be a big help. She seems absolutely devoted to him. She's always showing me a picture or telling me some story about him whenever I run into her," Greg assured Emily.

"Ready to eat?" Gabby interrupted, setting a large bowl of steaming mashed potatoes on the table.

Emily realized she was starving. In all the excitement, she hadn't had much time for food. That was a new one for her. Apparently finding dead bodies would be a benefit to her hips, if not her nerves. She couldn't wait to dig into those potatoes and one of the juicy pork chops staring at her from across the table. She managed to hold herself back while the twins said their version of grace, and then she pounced. She was about to shovel in the first mouthful when she once again heard her phone ringing from the other room. "Excuse me," she murmured and raced to the couch where she'd left her purse. One glance at her phone showed that it was her mom calling again. She answered at once.

Her mom always talked fast and furiously, but normally Emily could understand her. Not this time. "Mom, slow down. I can't understand a word you're saying." The line went silent and Emily thought her mom had hung up on her until she heard her dad's voice instead.

"Turn on the news. There's a breaking bulletin about the murder. And about Helen." Emily felt her dad's words plummet to the pit of her stomach and settle there like a rock. She grabbed the remote off the coffee table in front of her with shaking fingers and stabbed the power button. A cartoon blared out cheerful music while various animal-like characters frolicked in a meadow. It took Emily a minute to figure out how to get the right channel, but the minute she did, she saw that a news reporter was standing outside the high school. According to the shellacked blonde on-screen, Helen Burning was named as the prime suspect in Jim Layton's murder. The reporter went on to say that Helen was believed to be on the run. Pepper spray residue was found on the victim, and Helen was known to carry a canister, especially since she often went running alone. An anonymous source told police that Helen and Jim Layton, the victim, had been overheard arguing prior to his demise. The motive was mentioned as financial gain, as Layton's wallet and phone were missing, and his bank account had been cleared out late last night, in three-hundred-dollar increments. As anyone in Ellington knew, Helen was widowed young and never had any children. Like Emily, she was an only child, so she was the sole caretaker for her mother, who was now in a nursing home due to Alzheimer's. The bubbly blonde reporter tried to look serious as she announced that anyone who had seen or heard from Helen Burning was encouraged to call the number on the bottom of the screen. Emily had the urge to reach through the screen and pull out a handful of that coiffed and cemented hair.

Emily clicked off the TV and sank numbly onto the couch. It took her a few seconds to hear the faint sound of her dad calling her name. She put the phone back up to her ear. "You're still there? Sorry. Got caught up in the news. They can't be right, can they, Dad? What does Mom think?"

Before her dad could reply, Emily heard the sounds of a scuffle and then her mom's voice came back on the line. "Emily, there is no way that Helen had anything to do with that poor man's death! Something has happened to her, and we have to find her." At that point, she broke down in sobs, and the connection was broken.

Emily looked up to see Greg and Gabby staring at her from the doorway. "Well, what do you think?" she asked them.

"I think they're grasping at straws," Greg stated.

"Helen is innocent!" Gabby pounded the top of the chair she was standing behind for emphasis.

"I think so too," Emily declared, standing up. "We can't let Helen be railroaded like this. That so-called anonymous source had to be Barnes, and I think he's lying to cover his own tail."

"So, it's settled?" Gabby asked her. "We're officially on the case?"

Greg snorted. "Nancy Drew and her faithful sidekick." Emily blushed, remembering Tad saying much the same thing earlier.

This time, Emily flipped back her hair. "Well, if we're going to be Nancy Drew, I think it's only fair that we have her little blue roadster to tootle around in."

Greg laughed out loud. "Yeah, right. You'd wreck it the first day you had it."

Emily threw a couch pillow at him, but he ducked. Emily bowed her head in mock defeat. "You're probably right, Greg. But I can't be Nancy Drew anyway."

"Why not?" Gabby asked indignantly.

"I'd never fit into those little pencil skirts she was always wearing," Emily told her, patting her own ample hips.

Gabby threw the pillow back at her and caught Emily on the shoulder. "You better start running with me, then, because pencil skirts or no, starting tomorrow we *are* going to be Nancy Drews." So much for the mashed potatoes, Emily thought, taking in her best friend's perfectly toned body. She'd had twins, for goodness' sake! No one should be allowed to look that good. It wasn't fair to the rest of the female population.

Gabby watched her warily. "Why are you glaring at me like that? You don't want to be Nancy Drew?"

"Oh, I do, I do," Emily told her as she hauled her butt out of the plump couch cushions. "It's just that sometimes, even though you're my oldest friend and might-as-well-be sister, I really hate you."

Gabby didn't even bat an eye. "You don't hate me—you hate running. Hate the game, not the player." This time the pillow hit its mark—right between Gabby's eyes.

CHAPTER FOUR

Emily yawned so big her jaw cracked. She groped blindly in the fridge for her morning hit of caffeine. Popping the top, she glugged deeply. "Rough night?" a voice asked right next to her ear. Emily's eyes flew open and she saw Tad smirking at her. As usual, he was dressed in khakis with a crease so crisp it could slice paper. Today's button-down shirt was a deep blue that reminded Emily of ocean waves and starry skies. The color made Tad's eyes look even bluer than usual. Not that she noticed, of course. The same way she didn't want to reach up and brush his perennially too-long hair back from those gorgeous blue eyes. Okay, obviously she needed more caffeine. She gulped greedily from the can again, not bothering to answer Tad's question.

Dropping down on the top of the small conference table in the teachers' lounge, Tad patted the space beside him. Emily swatted his legs aside and settled in a chair instead. "I can't believe you don't know how to sit in a chair correctly," she told him.

Tad didn't budge. "Talk, Pit. Did you see the news last night? How're you doing?"

Emily stared into her now-empty can as if offended that it dared to be empty. "Yeah, I was at Gabby's. I stayed later than I planned because I couldn't bear going home, knowing that Helen wouldn't be next door. But I got to help with the twins' baths and then bedtime stories, so it was worth the late night." Tad smiled—he too had a soft spot for those little girls. What Emily didn't tell him was how she had cowered under her covers, even after double- and triple-checking the lock on every door and window. Somewhere around 1:00 a.m., she had finally managed to get engrossed in a mystery she had been waiting to read. She didn't know when she finally dropped off to sleep, but it felt like only seconds before her alarm was blaring. Emily loathed alarms with a passion that was rivaled only by her hatred of running.

"Oh, and get this," she told Tad. "Gabby called me at 6:00 this morning so that we could go for a run."

Tad practically snorted soda out of his nose. He well knew Emily's aversion to running, as he had tried to talk her into going with him several times too. "What'd you tell her?"

"That I would run when running shoes came in heels."

"And…" Tad prompted.

"She hung up on me," Emily admitted.

"So why running today? Special occasion?"

Emily debated how much to tell him, then decided he'd find out the truth eventually anyway. "We've decided that we have to find Helen. We know she's not guilty. Our plan is to visit Serenity Falls after school to see what we can find out. That's the nursing home where Helen's mother is a resident."

Tad frowned. "Be careful, Em. There's a murderer out there."

Emily grimaced. "As if I need to be reminded."

Tad stood and held out a hand to help her up. "Better head to the gym. The bell's gonna ring any minute." As they headed out, he added, "You still didn't tell me why you were going running. Conditioning for outrunning the bad guys?"

Emily attempted to bump his shoulder but got his arm instead. For the millionth time, she wished she were taller. "No, it's so I can fit into Nancy Drew's pencil skirts."

Tad looked Emily up and down. Emily tried not to maintain eye contact, but the unmistakable heat in Tad's eyes made it difficult. "I like you just fine in what you have on, Pit."

Now Emily looked down, taking stock of her outfit for the day—slim black pants, a tawny-colored sweater tunic, and leopard print heels, of course.

"Do I get to be a Hardy boy? You might need backup."

Emily smiled coyly, glancing up at him through her lashes, then replied, "Nope. You're on dog-sitting duty, remember?" When he frowned, she added, "And Tad, you're no Hardy boy." At his insulted look, she continued, "James Bond? Maybe. But definitely no Hardy boy."

"Remember, I like mine shaken, not stirred," Tad murmured in her ear as they approached the gym doors, and then he disappeared into the crowd. Emily fanned her overheated face as she took her own seat among the junior class.

* * *

Principal Matthews had decided that the best way to get things back on track at school was to start the day with an all-school assembly. That way everyone would hear the same information at the same time, hopefully eliminating rumors. He was standing behind a podium facing the bleachers, once again looking put together and in charge. His somber black suit and tie set the mood. Normally, teachers, especially those who were class sponsors, would be circulating among the students or giving them "the look" in order to get them to be silent. But as Emily looked around her section, most of them were staring at Principal Matthews or at the floor. A few were whispering, but the quiet, tense air in the gym made it clear that the loss of Coach Layton, especially in such a violent way, had devastated the entire student body. Emily wondered how Principal Matthews would address the students. How much would he tell them?

She didn't have to wait long to find out as the final bell rang, and Principal Matthews cleared his throat. The microphone on his podium gave a small squeal of feedback, but other than that, silence reigned. He began by talking about what a wonderful teacher and coach Jim Layton had been and how he knew they were all suffering from his loss. He hesitated a moment as sobs were heard from various sections of the bleachers. Emily wasn't sure what he would say about Helen, but she figured he would feel the need to address it somehow.

As if reading her mind, Principal Matthews continued. "I know many of you saw the news last night. I want to make it clear that no one, and I do mean no one, connected to the school thinks that Counselor Burning is guilty of any crime." He paused to closely scan the crowd, and Emily wondered if he was looking for Mr. Barnes. "However, the fact remains that we don't know Ms. Burning's whereabouts at this time. We have brought in several grief counselors for anyone who wishes to speak with them." He motioned to a row of men and women standing at the far end of the gymnasium. "I am truly sorry for the loss of our beloved coach. He was a good man. School will let out at noon tomorrow for his memorial service, as I assume many of you will want to attend. Any questions?"

Nathan, an avid football player and one of Emily's students, raised a tentative hand. When Principal Matthews called on him, he had to fight to keep his voice steady as he stood and asked, "What about our season? What do we do without Coach?"

Principal Matthews motioned to someone in the front row, and Assistant Coach Jerry Bly stood up. "Coach Bly will be taking over."

The young coach stepped up the podium and addressed his players. "I'm not even going to attempt the fill the shoes left behind by Coach Layton, but I do know that he would want you all to finish out the season, so let's do our best for him." A few halfhearted cheers greeted Bly's words. He continued, "Out of respect for Coach Layton's memorial, we will not be playing this Friday night. Practices will resume their normal schedule starting on Monday."

As Emily watched the newly promoted coach take his seat, she noticed Stevie a few rows below her. Even from her position, Emily could see that he was battling tears. Her heart broke for him. She once again made a mental note to call his mom during her conference period to reschedule their meeting. After a few more questions from students, Principal Matthews dismissed the group to head back to class.

It was a solemn group that moved through the halls. Emily passed by the side stairs and took the long way around so as to avoid the copy room. She still hadn't made copies of that quiz, but she didn't think the students were really up for one anyway. Emily sent a few students at a time to talk with the waiting grief counselors throughout the class period. Wanting to give the students an additional outlet for their confusion and sadness, she let the students spend the class period journaling about their reactions to losing Coach, Counselor Burning's disappearance, or anything else that came to mind. The same pattern continued with each class until lunch. Emily had been relieved to get out of her classroom, but she found that the same oppressive air weighed down the teachers' lounge also. Emily raised her eyebrows at Tad. He got the hint, and they slipped out of the lounge to eat in Tad's room instead.

"How're your students doing?" Emily asked over a mouthful of leftover mashed potatoes from dinner at Gabby's the night before.

"Quiet. Hard to get much done, but I think it's good to at least provide them with some structure." Tad toyed with the pile of grapes he had beside him. "I've been thinking about you and Gabby going to Serenity Falls after school. Do you really think that's a good idea?"

Emily slowly set down her fork. "What exactly are you trying to say, Tad?"

He held up his hands in surrender. "I'm saying that I'm worried. I don't want you to get hurt." Emily could see from the genuine worry in his eyes that he was telling her the truth, but she was afraid that would just have to be Tad's problem. No one told Emily Taylor what to do.

Tad saw the battle light in her eyes. He gave a huge sigh and munched on a grape. "You're going anyway, right?"

"Yep," Emily answered. "Sorry, Tad, but I will not sit back and let someone I care about get blamed for a crime I am positive she didn't commit. Frankly, I'm surprised you'd want me to." Emily wasn't sure if it was anger or disappointment that held the upper hand as she stared a hole through Tad's bent head.

He ate another grape, avoiding her eyes. "I want to find Helen and prove her innocence every bit as much as you do. But this is serious, Em."

"I know that, Tad. But I also know I can take care of myself."

Tad never had time to answer as the bell signaling the end of lunch rang. Emily brooded over what Tad had said throughout her entire next class period. What kind of trouble did he think they might get into? Did he think the murderer was hiding out at a nursing home? That he might throw off his disguise, leap from his borrowed wheelchair, and attack her in plain sight of dozens of witnesses? By the time her conference period rolled around, Emily was positive that Tad's worries were unfounded. Once again determined to get to the bottom of things, Emily pulled up Stevie's contact information and headed to the phone in the lounge. While she couldn't launch her investigation into Helen's disappearance until after school, she could take some steps toward figuring out what was troubling Stevie Davis.

Emily tried the home number that was listed first, but when no one answered, she figured Arlene was probably at work at this time of day. She looked up the number for Masterson Real Estate. The perky secretary who answered told her that Arlene had just left to show a couple a house, but Emily might be able to catch her on her cell phone. Deciding that Stevie's success in school was important enough to bother Arlene while she was working, Emily dialed Arlene's cell. The phone rang and rang. Emily was mentally composing the voice mail message she planned to leave, so she was startled when a harsh voice grated in her ear. "Hello?"

Emily stared at the phone in her hand, checking to make sure she'd dialed the right number. "Arlene Davis?" she asked.

"Yes. Who's this?"

Emily was taken aback. She had the right number, so obviously this was Stevie's mom. Her demeanor over the phone left Emily doubtful as to how much help she could actually provide though.

"Uh, I'm Emily Taylor, your son Stevie's English teacher? We had an appointment to meet the other day, but I had to cancel?" Emily realized all of her sentences were coming out as questions and mentally straightened her spine. She had dealt with rude and unhelpful parents before. She had this. Piece of cake.

"Oh, yes, Ms. Taylor, I meant to call you to reschedule but assumed you would need some time to get back into the swing of things after what happened." Once again, Emily pulled the phone back to stare at it in bewilderment. Gone was the harsh, abrupt woman of moments before. In her place was a solicitous, helpful parent. Emily was never one to look a gift horse in the mouth, so she plunged ahead.

"We have had a hard day, but I'm even more concerned about Stevie, knowing he was close to Coach Layton. I sense that Stevie has the ability to do the work—he just lacks the motivation. Any chance we could reschedule that meeting for sooner rather than later? Is there a day next week that would work for you?"

"How about tomorrow?" Arlene countered. "My Stevie is truly a brilliant child. I think if we put our heads together, we can figure out a way to motivate him, don't you?" Emily had yet to say a word, but Arlene continued. "Stevie is one in a million. I am truly blessed. I would do anything in my power to help him succeed."

"Great!" Emily was thrilled to hear that Arlene was as concerned about Stevie as she was. "I would be happy to meet with you tomorrow before school."

"I don't think we'll have to cancel for the same reason this time." Arlene tried to laugh, but it was a weak attempt at humor and they both knew it. Arlene tried to cover up her gaff by saying, "I look forward to meeting with you, Ms. Taylor. Stevie loves to read and is an exceptional writer."

"I look forward to hearing more about that," Emily assured her. "Stevie's work and attention have been lackluster in both areas thus far."

"This move has been hard on him. I think maybe—look, I hate to cut you short, but I need to get back to work. See you tomorrow." And with that, Arlene hung up.

Emily was still staring at the phone in her hand like it was a foreign object when Tad sauntered in. "What'd that phone ever do to you?" he asked.

Emily gazed up at him, confusion written all over her face. "I just had the strangest conversation with Arlene Davis. She went from rude to friendly, then when I suggested we meet next week, she wanted to meet tomorrow. We were discussing Stevie when she abruptly said she had to get back to work and hung up."

"So what's so strange about that?" Tad asked, grabbing a soda from the fridge. He waggled one at Emily and she nodded. He joined her at the table, adding, "She was probably meeting clients and had to hang up when they arrived."

It was a reasonable explanation, but Emily couldn't shake the feeling that Arlene Davis had sounded not only busy, but oddly harassed. Maybe she's high strung, she decided as the bell rang, and she and Tad headed back to their respective classrooms to finish up the longest school day in recorded history.

CHAPTER FIVE

———

As the final bell of the day rang, Emily pushed and jostled her way out the door right along with the students. She tried to stay in the middle of the pack and walk on her tiptoes so that her heels wouldn't be heard. A few of the students gave her funny looks, but most were more concerned about getting out of school for the day. Emily was hoping for a clean getaway from Tad—she was not in the mood for another lecture. At the top of the back staircase, Emily saw Gabby's maroon minivan idling outside. Taking the stairs two at a time, she charged through the double doors like a running back about to score a goal. She didn't stop sprinting until she was safely in the vehicle, with the door shut and locked, for good measure. She was too busy checking over her shoulder to notice that Gabby was staring at her like she had two heads.

Emily whipped around when she realized they weren't moving. "Go!" she shouted.

Gabby put the minivan in gear but was careful to mind the posted speed limits, as the school resource officer, Deputy Carson, was keeping a sharp eye out. Emily strained against her seat belt as if willing them to move faster.

"Who are you looking for?" Gabby finally asked. "You jumped in here like it was your getaway car. And since I know you didn't rob a bank, am I to assume that you have suddenly joined the cult of minivan lovers?"

Emily shot her an *oh, please* look. She and Gabby had always laughed at minivan-driving soccer moms, but as soon as Gabby found out she and Greg were having twins, a minivan seemed to be the only way to go. Gabby had not gone willingly to the dark side at first, clinging to the two-door-sports-car life she had led up to that point. But now, with two car seats strapped in the back, Gabby had embraced the cult wholeheartedly, even down to the little vinyl stick-person family on the back window. Emily loved Gabby and the girls unconditionally, but a minivan? No way. No how.

"For your information, I was trying to avoid having to talk to Tad again today. He thinks we're in over our heads and shouldn't be going out to Serenity Falls."

"Well, tough toenails. We're going anyway." Emily smiled. This was the Gabby she knew, the one who wouldn't let anyone tell her what she could or couldn't do. "And I brought you a snack," Gabby continued.

Emily took in the crushed Cheerios and leftover juice-filled sippy cups behind her and felt her stomach turn over.

"Not back there, silly. Here." Gabby motioned to the console. One would have thought she'd been handed diamonds the way Emily squealed over the large soda with a red straw and the Snickers bar beside it.

She had taken her first gooey bite of chocolate heaven when a thought occurred to her. "Are you bribing me so I'll run with you?" Emily narrowed her eyes at Gabby and took another defiant bite.

"Is it working?" Gabby asked, batting her eyelashes.

"No, and here is where we turn." Emily pointed out the tall stone columns that marked the entrance to Serenity Falls.

Emily took in the massive stone and wood building as Gabby pulled into a parking spot reserved for visitors near the front doors. They both stared out the windshield, awed by the grandeur of the facility. Gabby let loose a low whistle and turned to Emily. "This place looks more like a fancy resort than a nursing home."

Emily nodded in agreement. Even with a name like Serenity Falls, she had pictured a typical single-level, utilitarian-looking facility. In front of her, massive wood beams framed the three-story complex, floor-to-ceiling windows reflecting back the cloudy sky. Emily licked the last of the chocolate from her fingers and shot Gabby a grin. "Let's go check it out."

Gabby practically bounced on her toes as she locked the minivan and fell into step beside her. "Our first mission," she whispered.

Emily smothered a laugh as she pulled open one of the behemoth, carved wooden doors. The lobby they entered was as impressive as the outside suggested. The ceiling soared straight up three floors, skylights flooding the rich, dark wood floors with warmth and light, despite the lack of sunshine outside. A miniature waterfall provided a continuous murmur, inviting visitors to stop and rest in one of the cozy seating areas arranged throughout the large space.

Gabby pulled her toward the highly polished wooden counter discreetly tucked in the opposite corner. Emily checked to make sure her jaw wasn't hanging open as they approached the receptionist, a shy-looking blonde with large, round glasses, who asked, "Welcome to Serenity Falls. How may I assist you today?"

Emily checked the blonde's name tag and replied, "Hi, Shelley. We're friends of Helen Burning. As you may have heard on the news last night, it appears Helen is missing. I know she visited her mother here every day, so I was wondering if anyone had seen her recently."

Shelley's hair fell over one eye as she shook her head. With an impatient gesture, she jerked a hair band off her wrist and twisted her hair back. "No," she told them as she worked on securing her ponytail. "I haven't seen her the last two days, and I've been working both afternoons. She always comes by after school and sometimes before school as well. I checked with Jan, the one who works mornings," she explained, "and she hasn't seen her either." Shelley pushed her glasses up on her nose, looking worried. "Where is she?"

Gabby reached over and patted her hand. "We're not sure. But we'll find her. I promise."

Emily nodded gamely, but she didn't feel half the assurance Gabby displayed. "I take it this is unusual behavior for Helen?"

"Absolutely!" Shelley was emphatic. "Mrs. Quinton is the most visited patient we have. Helen dotes on her mother. Yesterday was one of Mrs. Quinton's good days, and she kept coming up to ask when her daughter would be here. It broke my heart." Shelley tugged at a loose thread on her turquoise cardigan.

"Would it be okay if we visited Mrs. Quinton?" Gabby asked.

Shelley brightened at the suggestion but was quick to add, "Today has not been one of her better days. Still, I'm sure she'd appreciate the visit." Shelley directed them toward a hallway farther past the receptionist's counter. Mrs. Quinton had a room on the first floor, facing the back grounds. Emily and Gabby found her sitting in a comfortable armchair in front of a big picture window that overlooked a much larger version of the waterfall from the lobby. Its muted crash was a soothing sound. Gabby knocked gently on the open doorframe, and they were waved forward by an imperious-looking hand. As they entered, Emily saw that Mrs. Quinton was working on a complicated jigsaw puzzle of Big Ben. The elderly woman fit her piece in place and smiled triumphantly up at them. "Well, don't just stand there," she commanded them. "Pull up a couple of chairs." They did just that, taking in the separate bedroom and bath as well as the small electric fireplace glowing in the corner. Emily's mind boggled at what it must cost to live here—surely more than she could make in a year. As an only child, she hoped her parents didn't expect to end up somewhere like this if they needed assisted living. They'd have to settle for her tiny spare bedroom.

Gabby chatted with Mrs. Quinton about her puzzle. Apparently, Mrs. Quinton had spent some time living in London when she was a newlywed. Emily tried not to be jealous, looking at where the dignified older woman was now. Mrs. Quinton reminded Emily of an old-fashioned schoolmarm. Her white hair was wound in a neat bun. A pair of half spectacles dangled from a chain around her neck, and she sat ramrod straight, both of her orthopedic shoes planted firmly on the carpet. Despite the warmth of the room, Mrs. Quinton had an afghan over her legs and a sweater thrown over her shoulders. Emily listened to Gabby engage the woman in further conversation, searching for a place to bring up the topic of Helen. Mrs. Quinton, however, took the matter into her own hands. Looking right at Emily, she said, "Helen, you've put on some weight. I thought you were taking up running."

Gabby smothered a laugh with a cough. Emily struggled not to be insulted. She could see where Mrs. Quinton might confuse her with her daughter. They both had cropped, brunette hair and were short in stature. Emily had to grudgingly admit that Helen was skinnier than her due to the fact that she was, indeed, an avid runner. Helen also sported a pixie cut rather than Emily's longer bob and was more than twenty-some years older, but Emily decided it would be easier to go with it rather than try to correct Mrs. Quinton. She didn't want to confuse her further. "I'm sorry, Mother. Work has been piling up. I'll start running more soon."

Mrs. Quinton gave a regal nod. "That would be best, Helen dear. Our health should be one of our most guarded treasures." Emily nodded mutely. She and Gabby exchanged a look and Emily knew they were both thinking what a fragile thing health really was. Mrs. Quinton had clearly taken good care of her physical body, but her mind had had other ideas. They watched her work on her jigsaw puzzle for a while. She seemed to have forgotten the girls were there. The fire at her back was making Emily feel drowsy. She was wondering if they should even bring up Helen or slip quietly out of the room, when Mrs. Quinton looked up at her again.

"Oh, there you are, Helen. I was just asking that sweet receptionist when you were going to get here. Did you get the money?"

Emily and Gabby both scooted forward in their seats, excitement vibrating between them. Maybe they would find out something about Helen's whereabouts after all. "What money, Mother?" Emily asked quietly.

Mrs. Quinton started to answer and then stared at Emily blankly. Her eyes went from sharp and inquisitive to cloudy and unfocused. She reached over to grasp Emily's hand. Emily gripped her cool, gnarled hand. "I'm sorry, dear," the older woman looked at her with a confusion that broke Emily's heart. "Who did you say you were again?"

Emily answered gently, "We're friends of your daughter, Helen."

"Helen? I had a daughter named Helen. She was such a good daughter, always taking care of me." And with that, Mrs. Quinton went back to her puzzle. Emily locked eyes with Gabby, wondering if they should question her further or leave quietly. Gabby shook her head and motioned to the door.

Emily hesitated. She hated to leave Mrs. Quinton alone. Sure, she was in a wonderful facility, but if they didn't locate Helen, what would happen to her? Emily stooped to kiss her wrinkled cheek. Mrs. Quinton looked up at her with eyes that no longer viewed reality. She patted Emily's hand. "You're a good girl, Helen," she said softly.

Emily and Gabby were both silent as they left Serenity Falls. Shelley hailed them on their way out and asked if Mrs. Quinton was having a good day. Gabby told her that Mrs. Quinton had thought Emily was her daughter and asked Shelley to please contact them if anyone at the facility heard from Helen. Shelley promised to let them know, taking down their names and numbers.

Back in the minivan, Emily stared at the leaden sky, which looked as heavy as her heart felt. Gabby started the ignition and said, "Well, that was certainly—"

"Depressing," Emily finished for her.

"Actually, I was going to say enlightening," Gabby corrected her. Emily slurped her soda, which was now watered down, and stared at Gabby.

"How so?" she asked.

"The money!" Gabby's eyes were shining with excitement, but Emily was not on the same wavelength.

"The money? Oh, you mean when Mrs. Quinton asked Helen—I mean, me as Helen—about whether she had gotten the money?"

"Of course." Gabby nodded, turning on the wipers, as the first raindrops began to splatter her windshield. "It makes perfect sense."

Emily chewed on her straw, trying to puzzle out what Gabby was seeing that she wasn't. "I assumed her comments were part of the ramblings of a deteriorating mind. I take it you didn't?"

"No, not at all. Did you see that place? It has to be costing Helen a fortune to keep her mom there. Where is she getting that kind of money? Not from being a counselor at the local high school, unless you guys have suddenly gotten astronomical raises." She quirked an eyebrow Emily's way. Emily merely snorted. "That's what I thought. So Helen had to be getting the money from somewhere. She disappeared the same evening Jim Layton was killed. What if Helen was blackmailing Jim? Maybe she threatened to turn him over if he didn't pay up, and when he still refused, she snapped and killed him." Gabby looked quite smug about her deductive reasoning capabilities.

Emily almost hated to burst her bubble as she said, "But that doesn't make sense. If Helen was blackmailing Jim, she wouldn't kill off her money source. It would be more likely that Jim would hurt Helen to get her off his back. And for that matter, what could Helen possibly have on Jim anyway?"

Gabby pouted. "You're right. I guess it doesn't make sense after all."

Emily reached over to hug her as they pulled back into the school parking lot. "I think you're right about the money being important, though."

"You do?" Gabby looked hopeful again.

Emily nodded, climbing out of the minivan into the drizzling rain. "Want to do some checking and see how much it would cost to house someone at Serenity Falls?"

"Absolutely! I'll call you tomorrow. Right now I have to go get the twins before they tie Greg's mom into a pretzel." But Gabby waited until Emily was safely in her own car before pulling out of the now-empty lot. Gabby turned one way. Emily went the other.

* * *

There was no one waiting for Emily at home. Helen and Duke weren't even next door. Her mind was spinning with ideas of money and blackmail and murder, all of which still seemed surreal. Not ready to be alone with her thoughts, Emily changed course and swung by her parents' house instead.

Parking in front of the large, pale-yellow Victorian home in which she'd been raised, Emily felt a glow of pride. She'd loved growing up in this big, old, creaky house that always needed something fixed. Even as a child, Emily had stared at her walls at night, painted a periwinkle blue back then, and wondered what stories this house could tell. Smiling to herself, knowing she had never let go of that childhood notion, she let herself in the back kitchen door. Something burbled on the stove. Pausing, she took a long sniff. Yum…Dad's chili. Maybe she could wrangle an invitation to dinner. Taking the two steps down into the family room, Emily saw her mother seated in her favorite rocking chair. Her head was bent over her work, the floor lamp behind her casting her in a pool of light. So intent was she on her clacking knitting needles that she didn't even notice Emily until she plopped down on the couch across from her. Glancing up, her mom dropped her knitting and pressed a hand to her heart.

"Em! You scared me."

"Sorry, Mom. I assumed you heard me come in the kitchen door." Emily was surprised at her mom's reaction. She had never known her mom to be scared of anything. Just went to show how murder in a small town like theirs could put everyone on edge.

"Have you heard anything from Helen?"

"No, but I was hoping maybe you had." Emily hated to see her mom hurting like this, but she had to ask her some tough questions.

Emily scooted forward on the couch, looking her mom in the eye. "I have to ask you something that might upset you. Gabby and I went out to Serenity Falls today to see if we could find out anything about Helen." Her mom's eyes glowed with hope. But as Emily continued, that glow faded. "Helen has not been seen there for the past two days, which is obviously out of character. We visited with Mrs. Quinton and, in what appeared to be a fairly lucid moment, she asked me if I had the money."

Her mom gave her a blank stare. "Mrs. Quinton doesn't even know you, Emily, so why would she be asking you about money?"

Emily fidgeted in her seat. "Well, that's the thing. She kind of thought I was Helen?" Her statement came out sounding more like a question.

Her mom surged to her feet. "You pretended to be her own daughter?"

Emily hopped up too. "No, Mom! It wasn't like that. She mistook me for Helen." Her mom didn't answer, but she stormed up the steps into the kitchen. Giving the chili a violent stir, she turned to glare at Emily. It was clear she knew there were more disturbing questions to come.

Hanging back in the doorway, Emily quietly asked, "Is there any way Helen could have been blackmailing someone, Mom? Someone like Coach Layton?" At her mom's narrowed eyes, Emily rushed on. "I mean, have you seen Serenity Falls? It must cost Helen a small fortune to keep her mother out there. She had to be getting the money from somewhere."

Her mom sighed, leaning back on the counter beside the stove. "Em, I don't know what to think anymore. I never thought my own daughter would find a dead person in the school where she grew up and now teaches. Life is full of surprises. But Helen as a blackmailer? She's a proud woman and probably wouldn't have asked for help even if she needed it, but you know as well as I do that Helen is as ethical as they come."

Emily moved forward and hugged her mom. "I do know that, Mom, but I had to ask. I hope you understand." When her mom finally hugged her back, Emily assumed all was forgiven. Taking one last longing look at the chili, Emily decided it would be best if she headed home. Giving her mom one last squeeze, Emily slipped out the back door. Twilight had settled over the backyard, but a light was shining in her dad's small workshop. Making a quick detour, Emily cut across the yard to see what new project her dad was working on.

Pushing open the door, she inhaled the scent of sawdust. It was a smell she had always associated with her dad. He had piddled in woodworking out in the garage all the years he had taught, but when he finally retired, he set up shop back here in his own space. Emily suspected that this place was also his refuge from some of her mom's zanier craft projects. Her dad finished sawing through a board, the whine of the saw reverberating in the small room. Then he pushed his safety glasses up on his head and said, "Hey, Pumpkin! What brings you by?"

He held out his arms for a hug, and Emily stepped into his warm embrace. She had always been daddy's little girl, and she wasn't ashamed to admit it. "I was quizzing Mom about Helen." At her dad's puzzled frown, she told him about her and Gabby's trip out to Serenity Falls.

When she'd finished, her dad scratched his chin. "Sounds like the money has to figure in somewhere, but if you truly believe Helen's disappearance is tied to the coach's death, doesn't it make more sense to me to dig into his past rather than Helen's?"

Emily stared bug eyed at her dad. Was he honestly encouraging her to investigate a murder? Seeing her look of disbelief, he hastened to add, "I mean, I don't want you physically involved in any sort of investigation. I just meant doing some Internet research. Theodore is excellent at ferreting out such information." And there it was. Once again, her dad was pushing her toward Tad. Emily started to make a sarcastic comment but then stopped to consider what her dad had said. Researching Jim did make sense, and Tad *was* a computer nerd.

"Okay." She shrugged at her dad. "I'll ask him tomorrow at school."

Her dad examined the board he had cut. "Or you could call him now," he suggested. Emily rolled her eyes and dropped a quick kiss on her dad's stubble-covered cheek.

"I'll keep you updated," she called over her shoulder, once again stepping out into the night. The first stars were pushing through the navy velvet of the sky, and the moon looked hazy behind its thin veil of clouds. Emily headed toward her car, pulling her phone from her pocket. Enjoying the cool night air, she paced the sidewalk, where she had punished her knees and elbows while learning to roller-skate and ride her bike, waiting for Tad to pick up. When he finally did, he sounded out of breath.

"Hey, Pit," he panted.

"Am I catching you at a bad time?"

"No, I just got back from a run and was headed to the shower."

Heat flooded Emily's face at the thought of Tad in the shower. Naked. Steamy. And where had that come from? Thankful Tad couldn't see her, she stammered, "Okay, good, well, I'll keep this short." She commanded herself to get it together, listening to Tad's low chuckle. "As you know already, Gabby and I went out to Serenity Falls this afternoon." Tad gave a small grunt, but Emily steamrolled right over his disapproval, explaining what they had found. "So"—she paused for a second—"I was wondering if you could help me by doing some research into Jim's past," she said in one breath.

"Sure," Tad replied, and Emily let out a whoosh of relief. "On one condition," he continued. Uh-oh. Emily frowned at the phone in her hand.

"What condition?" she demanded suspiciously.

"You come over to dinner in a couple of hours so we can discuss what I find."

Caught off guard, Emily mumbled, "Okay." Then, straightening her shoulders, she asked, "What can I bring?"

"Nothing. I've got everything I need. You can help toss the salad when you get here." Before Emily could agree, or even respond, the line went dead and Tad was gone. She might not be getting her chili, but she was still getting dinner, so she guessed a gal couldn't complain.

CHAPTER SIX

———

Stepping out of the shower, Emily could feel the silence wrap around her like a blanket. Normally, she found such silence soothing, like a favorite quilt she could wrap herself up in and feel safe. But knowing that Helen was missing and Jim was dead, the silence felt like it was smothering her, a sheet covering her eyes and ears. She turned up the music on her iPod to penetrate the silence and then stood staring into her closet.

After a few minutes of unproductive shuffling of the hangers, she gave up and called Gabby, who sounded breathless and frustrated.

"Hey! I haven't had a chance to look into the cost of Serenity Falls yet. The girls have been—" Emily heard loud barks resonate down the phone line. "Sorry, Em. As I was saying—Abigail and Phoebe, you leave that poor dog alone right now!" Emily was about to offer to call back later when she heard a rich baritone in the background.

"Ah, Greg's home. He can have his turn with the little tormentors. I'm all yours. What's up?"

"I wasn't calling about Serenity Falls, though we do need to look into that. I was actually looking for an emergency consult."

Emily could practically feel Gabby's shoulders snap to attention. "What for—hair? Shoes? Clothes? Men? Murder?"

Emily laughed and realized it felt good to do so. "Clothes. I'm meeting Tad at his place for dinner, and…You'd better not be giggling, Gabriella Marie," Emily warned.

Gabby cleared her throat. "Of course not. Please continue."

Emily ignored her continued snickers. "Anyway, we're meeting to discuss some research into Jim's past that he's doing for us. So do I dress professionally? Casually? What?"

Emily and Gabby debated nearly the entire contents of her closet before Emily settled on a pair of dark skinny jeans, a turtleneck sweater, boots (with heels, of course), and dangly earrings. Emily finished off her look with smoky eye makeup, dark lipstick, and perfume. Some mousse and backcombing gave her shiny bob some volume. Strapping on her favorite watch, Emily noticed she still had plenty of time before she had to leave for Tad's. Knowing that if she settled down to watch some TV she would end up gnawing off her lipstick, Emily grabbed her favorite confidante, her journal, and headed to her breakfast nook, which had always been her favorite place to write.

Those close to Emily considered her journal writing a type of obsession. She had an entire shelf in her office dedicated to the journals she had kept over the years. She didn't think of her writing as a compulsion but rather as a way for her to process information. She thought things through more clearly by writing them down, and right now, she had plenty to puzzle over. After scribbling several pages about the events of the last few days, Emily reviewed what she had written. Chewing on the end of her pen, she considered what questions she still had concerning Jim's death and Helen's disappearance. She listed them:

1. Where's Helen?
2. Did Helen need money badly enough to blackmail someone?
3. Who could Helen have been blackmailing? Jim? About what?
4. Could Helen have killed Jim?
5. Could the money mentioned by Mrs. Quinton be simply the ramblings of an addled mind?
6. Who would have known that Jim would be at the school that late?
7. How did Mr. Barnes afford that fancy car??

Emily knew she might be fixating on Barnes because she disliked him so much, but the timing of his new car ate at her. She had a sudden flashback from *Varsity Blues,* in which the main character, Mox, asks the same question about his health teacher. Turned out she was a stripper on the side. Could Barnes be a stripper on the side? Emily shuddered and slammed her journal shut. Enough speculation for now. If she had to think of Barnes in a tiny Speedo, she'd lose her appetite for dinner.

* * *

Tad answered the door wearing a soft, gray sweater and jeans, with a dishtowel slung over one shoulder. Emily blamed her salivating on the smells that wafted from the kitchen. "Smells delicious," she said as Tad took her coat. "What can I do to help?"

Tad motioned to the salad makings laid out by the cutting board. "I thought you could work on the salad while I finish up the roast chicken and new potatoes." Emily was impressed. She loved to cook but had had no idea that Tad did too. When she mentioned that, he turned to her with a slow smile. "There are several things you don't know about me, Em." His eyes held hers so that her hand faltered on the knife she was using to chop up a red pepper. She was relieved when he turned back to the stove. Chopping off a finger would definitely put a damper on the evening. "I had an excellent wine picked out to go with the chicken but figured you'd probably prefer soda," he said over his shoulder.

Emily laughed at the cold, fizzy drink he set in front of her. "You know me well, Tad. You know me well."

Tad leaned in closer, their arms brushing as he whispered, "I do, Em. That I do." Emily would have sworn that electricity was snapping in the air around them. She felt her eyes drifting closed as she swayed imperceptibly closer to Tad. Then a furry head bumped her leg at the same time claws dug through the back of her jeans. She yelped and jumped back. Duke stood, giving her his "poor me" doggy eyes. She had completely forgotten about the tiny dog. Tad looked as rattled as she did as he bent to give Duke a good rub.

"Poor guy must be hungry," Emily managed irritably. "After all, it does smell amazing in here." Duke wagged his tail happily, and Emily glared at the little traitor. The moment between her and Tad dissolved into that abyss of lost chances.

Once they were settled at his small kitchen table, Tad started in on the research he had compiled so far on Coach Layton. Emily savored the moist chicken but was frustrated by how little Tad had been able to uncover. Apparently, Jim's electronic footprint only went back as far as eleven years ago. At that time, he was teaching and coaching in a small district in Iowa.

"So where was he before Iowa?" Emily asked again.

Tad ran a hand through his hair. "That's just it, Pit. I have no idea. There is nothing out there, at least that I can find, before he started teaching in Peculiar Bluffs, Iowa."

Emily fiddled with her fork. "You know that Principal Matthews would never hire someone he hadn't completely vetted. Jim had to have had references. Maybe some of those would lead us to where he was before Iowa?"

"Good idea," Tad replied, stacking their plates and carrying them into the kitchen. "I'll check with Mr. Matthews first thing in the morning. You up for dessert? I picked up a red velvet cheesecake at Mae's Bakery yesterday." Tad waved the familiar pink-and-white-striped box under her nose.

Emily closed her eyes and inhaled as Tad slid a slice in front of her. Mae's was one of her favorite places on Earth, and Tad knew it. Her eyes snapped open, but she waited to speak until she had shoveled in the first creamy bite of heaven. She tried to keep a tiny moan from escaping, but this was Mae's, for crying out loud. Tad was watching her carefully, his slice still untouched. Emily broke off a white chocolate curl from the top of her piece and pointed it at Tad. "How did you know I'd be here for dessert?" Her eyes narrowed, but Tad didn't squirm.

"I didn't. I had to go in to order some donuts for the Mathletes' meeting, and when I saw she had one of these babies in her cooler, I couldn't resist. Why?"

Emily became intensely interested in her cheesecake. Why was she always jumping to the conclusion that Tad was trying to flirt with her? How narcissistic could she be? It was too bad that jumping to conclusions didn't burn calories, she thought, or she could be as skinny as Gabby in no time. Ignoring Tad's question, Emily changed the subject. "What about the social media sites? Surely Jim had a Facebook page or a Twitter account or something."

Tad nodded. "He does have a Facebook page, but it's only a few months old." Emily blew her bangs off her forehead in a huff. "But," he continued, "his page did say that he was in a relationship with Stephanie Lowell."

"Who's she?" Emily asked. Knowing Tad, he already had that all figured out.

He did. "She's a personal trainer at Perfect Fitness." He smirked at her. "I thought we could swing by there after the memorial service tomorrow and see what we can find out."

Emily groaned and dropped her head to the table. "Why couldn't she have been a chef? Or a clothing designer?" She knew she was perilously close to whining, but she didn't care. Of the top ten things she hated most in life, gyms rated right up there with mornings and running.

Tad had moved back to the kitchen and was running hot water in the sink to start washing dishes. Emily hurried to help him, but he shooed her away. "I'll do the dishes—you agree to go to the gym with me."

Emily crossed her arms in front of her. "Only in the name of research," she finally groused, taking a seat at the counter. "And speaking of research, don't you think we should check further into Mr. Barnes?"

Tad had pushed his sleeves up past the elbows, and Emily was trying not to notice the fine, dark hairs glistening on his forearms as he plunged his hands in the soapy water. Who knew doing the dishes could be so sexy? To detract attention from her heated face, Emily continued. "There's no way he could afford that car on our salary. What if he's like that Miss Davis in *Varsity Blues*?"

Tad frowned at her, trying to recall the reference. "You know, the sex ed teacher who was a stripper on the side?" she said to jog his memory.

The plate Tad was drying nearly crashed to the floor. "Are you suggesting Mr. Barnes is a stripper?" He stacked the last plate carefully in the cabinet before coming around to sit beside her. "That has to be the most ridiculous, and truly nightmare-worthy idea, I have ever heard you come up with."

The look of horror in Tad's eyes tickled Emily's funny bone. A giggle slipped out, and when Tad chuckled in return, Emily let loose with a full-out laugh that ended in her gasping for breath. The laughter eased the tension in her shoulders, and as Emily brushed her hair out of her eyes, she realized she was practically sitting in Tad's lap. She straightened so quickly, she banged his chin with the top of her head. Tad quit laughing and rubbed his jaw.

"I'm so sorry," Emily gushed, hopping up and dragging on her coat that had been left draped over the back of the couch. "One of the hazards of being short, I guess." She carefully buttoned every button on her coat, unsure of what to say or do next. Tad wasn't helping alleviate her awkwardness either. He stood casually in front of the door, her only means of escape. Terrified of making another stupid move, Emily blurted, "Thanks for dinner. And the research skills. We'll plan on the gym tomorrow."

Tad smiled at the grimace she couldn't quite mask at the mention of the gym. "You're welcome. It's a date, then." When he still didn't move, Emily took a hesitant step forward. Tad must have had the same idea she did because they collided a foot from the door. Trying not to lose her balance, Emily gripped Tad's waist. His arms came around her to steady her, and they shared an awkward hug. Emily never raised her eyes from his chest, but instead, she turned and darted out the door with a hastily called "thanks again" over her shoulder.

* * *

All the way home, Emily kicked herself for the way she had fumbled the good-bye at Tad's. What was wrong with her? She was a grown woman, not a hormone-addled teenager with a crush. They were working together, and that was it. At least that's what she told herself as she let herself into her duplex, but she knew what an awful liar she was.

Even though it was late, Emily picked up the phone to spill her guts to Gabby, hoping for some sympathy. Instead,

Greg answered, explaining that Gabby was busy rocking one of the girls who had woken up with a cough. Hearing how down she sounded, Greg offered to help, but Emily assured him that it was nothing but a silly girl problem and she would be fine. He reluctantly let her go, reminding her that all she had to do was call.

She settled for Bunny Tracks ice cream and old *Friends* reruns as her comfort instead. Yes, she had just had cheesecake, but she had to go to the gym tomorrow anyway, right? A commercial for an online dating service came on, and Emily briefly wondered if she should try something like that. It might be harder to embarrass herself over the Internet. Nah, with her track record, she could still mange it. Emily snuggled in the soft, maroon-and-navy throw blanket her mom had made her during her freshman year of high school, feeling sorry for herself. She changed the channel and came across a late-night marathon of *Golden Girls* reruns. Emily was chortling along with Dorothy, her favorite character, at one of Rose's silly stories, when it hit her—the *Golden Girls* were Helen's bedtime ritual. Emily often heard the theme song muffled through their joint walls when she was going to bed at night. The laugh died in her throat, and she stabbed the off button on the remote. Where could Helen be? Was she okay? Was she tied up in this mess of Jim's murder? And if so, how?

Since she had no answers, she could only pray that the morning would help to shed some light on these questions. Tossing the empty ice cream container in the trash, Emily shuffled down the hall to try and get some sleep. So what if she dragged her throw blanket to bed with her for comfort? No one was there to be the wiser.

CHAPTER SEVEN

After a restless night, punctuated by disturbing dreams combining Helen, the *Golden Girls*, and Jim, Emily finally fell into a sound sleep ten minutes before her alarm was set to go off. Emily slapped the offending clock hard enough to send it crashing to the floor and skittering under her bed. Pulling the covers over her head, Emily contemplated calling in sick to school. Mornings were number one on her list of "most hated things," so add to that the awkwardness she was sure to face with Tad, and the amount of sweets she had consumed last night with the looming dreaded trip to the gym, and she had the perfect recipe for a reason not to go to work. However, her desire to dig further into Jim Layton's past and help clear Helen's name was strong enough to propel her out of bed. Although the bags under her eyes were large enough to carry her papers to school in and dark enough to make her look like she'd gone a round with Mike Tyson, Emily was consoled by the new pair of gray suede ankle boots she finally had a chance to wear today. If there was a reason to get out of bed, for Emily, it was to wear a new pair of shoes.

Twenty minutes later, Emily stomped down the hallway toward her classroom, her boots making sharp staccato taps on the aged tile. She managed only to unlock her door and flip on the light before Tad stuck his head in the room. Emily immediately felt her face suffuse with heat, but in the quick glance she cast at his face, she was secretly delighted to see that his eyes looked as tired as hers. Not knowing how to break the silence, she merely shuffled papers around, searching for the folder she had put together for her meeting with Arlene.

Tad cleared his throat, but Emily didn't look up from her desk. Finally he said, "I went ahead and talked with Principal

Matthews about Jim this morning. I didn't expect you to be here this early."

Her head snapped up, and she glared in his general direction. Of course Tad would be here early enough to have taken care of business. She refused to give him the satisfaction of asking what was said, although she was itching to do just that. Instead she said, "I have an early meeting with Stevie's mother, remember?"

"Of course. Sorry," Tad mumbled, and Emily relented because Tad never mumbled. He clearly felt as awkward as she did. Last night had ended on a very strange note. Should she ask him about it, or ignore it and focus on the information about Jim? Tad settled the matter by saying, "Apparently, Jim came here with impeccable references from Iowa. He taught at Peculiar Bluffs for six years before coming to Ellington. Principal Matthews gave me a copy of his references if we want to contact them?" That final part came out as more of a question, and Emily pounced on it.

"Peculiar Bluffs is only, what, four and a half hours from here? Gabby and I could take a road trip and check things out in person." When Tad merely frowned, Emily rushed on, "In fact, I think I'll call her right now."

She snatched up her cell, pressing the speed dial number for Gabby and hoping that Tad would take the hint and leave. He didn't, instead leaning against the doorjamb in that careless, confident way of his. Emily turned her back on him, moving to the bank of windows on the opposite wall. She was relieved when Gabby answered on the second ring.

"Morning, Sunshine!" Emily chirped. "Hope I didn't wake you." She laughed, knowing her best friend was a notorious morning person. However, rather than the cheery reply she expected, Gabby only grunted.

"You okay?" Emily was immediately concerned.

Gabby yawned loudly. "Yeah," she mumbled. "Was up half the night with Phoebe. She had a bad cough."

"Is she okay?" Out of the corner of her eye, Emily saw Tad straighten up.

"She is. I think it's her allergies acting up. I took her in to Urgent Care first thing this morning, and they didn't think she needed any antibiotics. She's sleeping now."

"Sounds like you need to join her. But that's good news, at least. I can certainly relate on the allergy front." Emily waved at Tad, reassuring him that everyone was fine. He relaxed, but still didn't budge.

Gabby continued, "Greg said you called last night. Sorry I didn't get a chance to call you back. Did something happen, or not happen, at Tad's?"

"You know, Vicks on the feet, then cover with socks, really helps with the coughing. Mom used to do that to me all the time when I was a kid."

"Ah, message received. Tad's in the room with you, isn't he?"

"You betcha," Emily laughed.

"Well, I assume you're not calling to discuss the merits of Vicks, so what's up?"

"Actually, I was hoping to talk you into a road trip to Peculiar Bluffs."

"Iowa? How come?"

"Tad found out this morning from Principal Matthews that Jim taught and coached there before coming to Ellington. I'm hoping a quick trip up there could net us some more information to help find Helen and prove her innocence."

"Sure. You know me. I'm always up for a road trip. This can be our second mission."

Emily laughed at Gabby's whispery spy voice. "Great. We can leave after the memorial service today, if you want." Emily mentally crossed her fingers.

"Oh, no, Em. Sorry. I wouldn't want to head out until the morning. Just to make sure Phoebe does better tonight."

"Of course. I totally understand." But damn it all, now she didn't have an excuse to get out of going to the gym with Tad after Jim's service, after all. "I'll pick you up tomorrow. What time?"

"How 'bout seven?"

"In the morning?" Emily croaked. "It's a Saturday!"

"Early bird gets the worm and all that. See you tomorrow." And with a chuckle that sounded slightly sinister to Emily's jaded ears, Gabby hung up.

"Yeah. See you," Emily muttered, turning to see Tad flashing her a toothy grin.

"So we're still on for the gym today, right?"

Emily gave him a silent stare, palming the marble apple one of her students had given her last year. As if sensing her desire to bean him with it, Tad made a quick getaway.

Emily just had time to straighten up her desk and locate the file of materials she had put together on Stevie before Arlene Davis was knocking at her classroom door. Emily hopped up to greet the tall, lean woman, gesturing to a conference table at the back of her room. She preferred to hold conferences back there so that there wasn't the barrier of a desk between her and students or their parents, whichever the case might be.

Arlene took a seat, tucking her exquisite silver Coach purse under her chair. Emily, secretly lusting after that purse, said, "Thank you for coming in today, Ms. Davis."

"Please, call me Arlene," she replied with a careless wave of her hand.

Emily nodded, telling herself that it was ridiculous to feel intimidated by Arlene just because she looked so put together and polished. Or because she was tall enough that, even in her flats, she towered over Emily in her high-heeled boots. This was her domain. She knew her stuff. And they were both pursuing the same goal—to help Stevie.

Emily laid a piece of paper in front of Arlene. "This was the first major writing piece we did this year. The students were to pick a favorite object and then paint a picture of it with words. They were not to name the object in their writing. The average length was two full paragraphs, and as you can see..." Emily trailed off, watching Arlene read through the scant four lines in front of her. Emily could recall them completely without having to look at the page.

Arlene finally looked up, clearly baffled by her son's writing. "'I am brown. I have white laces. I spiral through the air. I am the reason for Stevie's existence.' Well, obviously he's talking about a football, but where's the rest of it?"

"That's it." Emily gestured toward the paper. "I asked him that same question myself, and he told me that was all he had to say."

Arlene's über-professional façade began to crumble slightly. As she reached for the second paper Emily removed from the folder, Emily noticed that her nails were bitten down to the quick. Real estate had to be a stressful job. "This was a personal narrative assignment. The students were to write about an event in their life that helped shape who they are today. Dialogue was to be included."

Arlene read the short paragraph, her fingers trembling slightly.

Moving to Ellington from my old school has completely changed my life. I had to leave all my friends and old football team behind. The best part about Ellington is Coach Layton. Football is my life even if my mom does say, "You spend too much time obsessing over football."

"I don't understand." Arlene flipped the page over as if looking for more, but there wasn't anything.

Arlene briefly pinched the bridge of her nose as if trying to relieve a headache. Emily's heart went out to this mom. Raising a child alone, being both mother and father, had to be one of the most difficult jobs in the world. When Arlene looked directly in her eyes, Emily saw the pain there and reached over to pat her nail-bitten hand. "Obviously," she began, "we both want the best for Stevie."

"Yes, yes, of course," Arlene agreed. "At first I *did* think it was football that was taking up too much of his time. But he does love to play. This move has been harder on him than I thought. But as a single parent, I have to go where the money is." She seemed to be pleading with Emily to understand. Emily nodded reassuringly and explained her plan to entice Stevie with a mythology unit.

"That sounds great." Arlene gave her a grateful smile. "I'll have a talk with him too, of course. Stevie is such a smart young man. He's always been a straight A student." Emily tried to hide her surprise at that tidbit of information. Arlene continued, "But I'm afraid the loss of Coach Layton is only going to make things worse."

"Yes, this has really rocked everyone's world. We all feel a bit off-kilter."

"I can't believe that Helen had such a capacity for violence. She was the first person in town to really befriend me. When I came up to the school to enroll Stevie, we discovered we were both avid runners. We've been on several runs and even caught a few movies together. I never would have suspected her." Arlene shook her head as if appalled by her supposed friend's murderous side.

Emily felt her hackles, whatever they were, rise. "I don't believe for one minute that Helen is guilty. She's a wonderful person. I, for one, want to find her safe and sound." Emily stood, signaling the end of their meeting. Her temper was about to boil over, and she knew the results would not be pretty.

Arlene looked slightly taken aback. "Of course, I'm sure you're right, Ms. Taylor. There has to be another explanation." Arlene pushed her own chair back so quickly that she knocked over the purse at her feet. Its contents spilled and scattered everywhere. Emily bent to help her, sorry she'd let her temper, always ready to blaze, fire up while with a parent. Hoping to smooth things over, she gathered up breath mints, a comb, and a compact. Arlene smiled her thanks, and Emily gave a tiny sigh of relief. Checking under the conference table to make sure they'd gotten everything, Emily saw a silver glint. She stretched and came out with a beautiful, enameled silver rectangle.

"How beautiful!" Emily exclaimed. "I don't think I've ever seen such a gorgeous lipstick case."

Arlene gave a light laugh as she tossed the case into her purse. "Yes, it is gorgeous, but it only poses as a lipstick case. It's actually pepper spray. I take it with me when I run. Supposedly, a would-be attacker would be more easily taken by surprise since it looks harmless enough. I can attach it to my keychain, too."

"That's a great idea," Emily enthused. "It's definitely less conspicuous than the bright-pink camo one I carry in my purse. But, of course, if you ever see me out running, it's because I'm being chased by an attacker anyway." Emily was trying to end the conference on a lighter note, reestablishing rapport with Arlene, but realized that in light of recent events, her attempt at humor fell flat. She tried again. "I sure wish the running bug would bite me. My hips would benefit for sure, but I'm afraid I remain bug free." She gave a rueful shrug.

Arlene smiled. "Once you're bitten, you never go back." She held out a hand. "Thank you for your time, Ms. Taylor. I'm sure between the two of us we can get Stevie back on track. There's nothing I wouldn't do for my son."

Emily saw Arlene to the door, hoping she was right. Arlene might be willing to do anything for Stevie, but Emily wondered if Arlene wasn't refusing to acknowledge how truly unhappy Stevie was here in Ellington. The first bell rang, and Emily put her worries about Arlene aside. Today was a short day due to Coach Layton's memorial service in the afternoon, and she had a hundred things to do before then.

* * *

Emily ran nonstop all morning, trying to get her students enthused about their new mythology unit. She felt like she had just gotten started when the final bell of the day rang. She dashed across the hall to the women's restroom to see how much her appearance had deteriorated since she'd left the house that morning. Her hair had only a few wayward wisps, and her makeup was mostly intact, so she considered herself good to go. Smoothing down the pearl-gray sweater dress she had paired with her new shoes, she decided she looked suitably somber. Taking one last calming breath, Emily headed out to make the short walk over to the football field where Jim's memorial service was to be held.

The bleachers were already packed by the time she arrived. The entire football team took up the first couple of rows. Emily climbed higher until she had a better view of everyone in attendance. She noticed that Pastor Dean was behind the podium placed down on the field. She enjoyed hearing Pastor Dean preach, as he had been her own pastor since she was young, but today she was more interested in observing than listening. She had read somewhere that killers often returned to the scene of their crime or showed up at the funerals of their victims. In this case, both were close at hand with the school on one side of the street and the football stadium on the other. Emily carefully scanned the faces of those in her near vicinity. She recognized most of the faces around her, even if she didn't know their names. One of the benefits of living in a small town. Detective Gangly-Arms was there, she noted. He was wearing a very ill-fitting suit, his cuffs showing at the end of each arm. He seemed to be intently observing faces, just as she was. She felt a small sense of triumph that she was on the right track, but her spirits fell again when she noticed Stevie seated across from her. He was clearly upset and swiping furiously at tears. Emily wondered why he wasn't sitting with the rest of the team. It was then she noticed Arlene beside him, a protective arm around his shoulders. Stevie shrugged her off, and Emily assumed that it was Arlene who had insisted Stevie sit with her.

She focused her attention back on the field as the school's jazz band played a haunting rendition of "Amazing Grace." Emily found herself furiously blinking back her own tears as the last notes lingered in the air. The band filed off the field, and Pastor Dean once again moved to the podium. He motioned to the large picture on an easel next to the podium. In it, Coach Layton had his arms raised in victory as his team emptied the contents of the water cooler over his head. Last year, the Eagles had been state champs. They had hoped to repeat that success this year. Emily thought the photo was a touching tribute, but she also wondered where Jim's remains would be buried, especially as he wasn't from this area originally. Pastor Dean addressed that very question, however, when he explained that police officials had yet to locate any surviving relatives. Emily leaned forward, anxious to hear any mention of where home had been for Jim Layton, but Pastor Dean did not give any further details.

Emily couldn't remember Jim ever having mentioned having any family before. She had known he wasn't married and didn't have any kids, of course, but she had somehow gotten the impression that he didn't really have any extended family either, as he never mentioned holiday plans or family visits. But then again, maybe Jim had been reluctant to discuss his personal life at school. While that was a foreign concept to Emily, whose life was an open book to anyone, it didn't mean other people couldn't keep things to themselves. She wondered if Jim had ever mentioned his hometown to Principal Matthews. She'd have to remember to ask Tad to check. She did another quick scan of the crowd for Tad's dark head but didn't see him.

Emily then focused on the service as several players and parents spoke highly of Coach Layton as a teacher, as a coach, and as a person. A couple of veiled references to the guidance or counseling he also gave to his players showed Emily that several people had already bought into the theory that Helen was responsible for the beloved coach's death.

Emily bowed her head for the final prayer by Pastor Dean. While her heart ached for the loss of Jim, her determination to locate Helen and figure out what had really happened that night was foremost in her mind.

As the crowd was dismissed, Emily stood, thinking to make her way down to Pastor Dean and thank him for officiating the service. While she waited for the crowd to thin, however, she noticed a tanned, blonde, Amazonian woman sobbing on the pastor's shoulder. By her sculpted legs and toned arms, Emily deduced she must be the girlfriend, Stephanie. She'd, unfortunately, get to meet her later at the gym.

The air of sadness and loss was beginning to smother Emily. Checking one more time for Tad, she skirted around the upper bleachers to exit on the other side. As she made her way along the clanging metal walkway, another man passed by ahead of her. Like her, he was moving on the fringes of the crowd. Unlike her, his head was down, and his shoulders were hunched as if he were trying to sneak away, not merely avoid the crowd. She was so intent on watching the man, she didn't pay close enough attention to where she was walking. Her shin banged into the bleacher next to her, sending reverberations throughout its length. The stranger jumped and glanced over his shoulder. Seeing Emily, he started to see her staring back at him and hurried away. In that moment, Emily felt a jolt of recognition. She was sure she had never seen that man before, yet he had seemed so familiar. Was her subconscious trying to tell her that this man was the murderer? Throwing caution to the winds, Emily hurried after the fleeing man with his suit coat flying out behind him. She gripped the stairway railing firmly so as not to lose her footing again. She moved as fast as her heeled boots would allow, but by the time she pounded down the last step, the man was nowhere in sight. Frustrated, Emily yanked down her sweater dress that had worked its way up during her mad pursuit. She reached up to smooth her hair, turning to head toward the school, and barreled into the people in front of her.

Emily immediately began to apologize, then saw that the person she had ran into was Arlene. The real estate agent waved off her apology, looking as composed as ever. Stevie, on the other hand, knuckled his red, swollen eyes, looking much younger than his seventeen years. Emily ached to hug him but knew that her motion would be rebuffed. Instead, she asked him if he planned to continue with football. Stevie's eyes brightened as he nodded. "Ms. Taylor, I love football. I don't think anything could make me quit." Here he glared at his mother, who still remained unfazed. Then his mouth and shoulders drooped again as he continued. "But it certainly won't be the same without Coach. I'm glad we don't have to play tonight. I don't think our hearts would be in it. It's too soon." He gave an awkward shrug. She wished again that there was some way she could help him. Arlene had a soothing hand on his arm, and Emily cast around for something to say that might cheer him up.

She shocked herself by what came out of her mouth. "Stevie, I know that you, and all the players, are hurting over this loss. I plan to do everything I can to see that justice is served. In fact, my friend Gabby and I are even headed up to Iowa tomorrow to see if we can find out anything that might help the investigation."

Emily wasn't sure if she was more surprised by her sharing of this information with Stevie or with his exuberant hug. "That's great, Ms. Taylor! I know you can figure this thing out and make sure that the evil SOB who did this is punished." He immediately turned a brilliant shade of red. "Begging your pardon for my language."

Arlene frowned, but Emily patted his hand. "It's okay, Stevie. I know you're upset. Hey, by the way, did Coach Layton ever talk about his past at all?" She knew it was a long shot, but she held her breath anyway.

"Not really. Coach was more 'all football, all the time.' Sorry." Emily pasted on a smile and thanked him anyway. "I'll see you Monday, Ms. Taylor. Thanks again."

"Yes, thank you," Arlene murmured as they passed.

Emily was berating herself for getting the boy's hopes up. What if she didn't find out anything useful? What if Coach Layton's killer was not found or brought to justice? She was lost in thought as she ambled toward the school and her car, so the light touch on her arm caught her by surprise.

"Tad! You scared me."

"You were so deep in thought I'm surprised you didn't wander into the street. Can't have my gym buddy getting hit by a bus, now can we?"

Emily groaned. It was official. This day could not possibly get any worse.

* * *

She grumbled all the way home. Digging to the very back of her closet, she unearthed the pair of running shoes she had purchased in a haze of New Year's Eve-resolution delirium. She didn't plan on actually doing any running, but they would work for the gym. At least they were cute, Emily consoled herself, as she tied the dark-purple laces. She surveyed herself in the mirror and shrugged. She had donned black yoga pants in hopes that the color would de-emphasize her hips. The long purple shirt she had paired with them was meant to conceal her hips if the black pants didn't help. She was heavily disappointed in the job both of them were doing, but Tad's insistent honking out front meant she had no time to change.

Tad gave her a huge grin as she climbed in the car, slamming the door behind her. When she remained silent, he laughed and turned on the radio. Emily refused to give him a chance to goad her, and so she said nothing until they had pulled up in front of the industrial-looking building that housed Perfect Fitness. Tad turned off the ignition and looked over at her. "Are you coming?" he asked her.

"Yes, but only because I'm worried about Helen. And"— she paused—"because I expect ice cream after this."

"After a workout?" Tad sounded incredulous, but Emily was sticking to her guns.

"Yep, after a 'pretend' workout, in the name of research."

"Have it your way, Pit." Tad locked the car, and they trooped into the gym. The industrial theme was carried into the interior as huge steel beams crisscrossed the soaring ceiling. Tad headed straight for the long concrete counter at the side of the room. Emily dragged her feet, taking in the stick-thin redhead behind it. She highly doubted that girl did any heavy lifting, which was what all the industrial elements made her think of. The redhead looked more like a poster child for bulimia or anorexia. Emily tugged the hem of her shirt even further down, trying not to snarl when Tad turned, holding out two visitor passes like he was offering her the world. Emily took the proffered pass, holding it away from her body as if it might bite, and followed Tad into a room filled with intimidating-looking machines. Terrified of losing a limb, or even worse, her dignity, Emily zeroed in on the one machine she knew how to use. Grabbing Tad's arm, she propelled him toward a row of treadmills.

She was feeling quite proud of herself once she was walking along at a fast clip, having figured the machine out all by herself. Then she glanced over and saw Tad jogging easily away on an incline much steeper than hers. She resisted, barely, the urge to push him off his own machine, but only because she was afraid to risk letting go of her own. Instead, she focused on the inspiring view in front of her of…the parking lot.

The day was overcast, and storm clouds appeared to be rolling in. A tall, blonde woman who had pulled into the parking lot was unfolding an umbrella. Emily looked closer at the blonde ponytail as it bobbed its way to the entrance. She was the Amazon from the memorial service. Emily tapped Tad, harder than necessary, and pointed her out. Tad nodded in acknowledgment, and they both slowed their machines, watching who had to be Stephanie make her way into the gym.

In moments, the woman, still in her sedate dress clothes, was making her way across the room, oblivious to the motion around her. Emily and Tad caught up to her right before she disappeared through a door that was clearly marked "Employees Only." Emily called out, "Stephanie?"

The woman turned, puzzled, and Emily could see that her eyes were red and swollen from crying. "Yes?" Her tone was cautious yet polite. Emily knew she was frantically trying to place them.

Emily saved her the trouble. "We're colleagues of Jim Layton. We taught with him at Ellington High. We are both so sorry for your loss." She motioned to both Tad and herself.

"I see. Well, thank you for your condolences." She began moving forward again, but this time Tad stopped her.

"We were wondering if we could speak to you a moment." Tad's voice was firm and encouraging. Stephanie looked them both up and down and then gave an imperceptible nod, motioning for them to follow her.

She led them through the employee door into a long hallway. Even more doors lined each side of the corridor. Stephanie unlocked the third one on the left, then waved them in ahead of her. Emily immediately felt claustrophobic in the small space. Seeing the panic in her eyes, Tad motioned her to the one visitor's chair, while he leaned casually by the door, propping it open. Stephanie plopped down in her own chair and dropped her head in her hands. "I don't mean to be rude," she began, "but as you know, it's been a very difficult day. I only came in to pick up a few demo Zumba tapes to preview over the weekend. What is it I can do for you?"

"Well—" Emily shot Tad a nervous look, and he nodded encouragingly. "—actually, we're trying to look into Jim's death a bit more. Helen Burning is a friend of ours, and we think the police are looking at the wrong suspect. We're hoping that maybe something in Jim's past could lead us to some new information."

Stephanie had stiffened at the mention of Helen's name, but since she didn't kick them out of her office, Emily was hopeful. She waited, giving Stephanie time to form a response. The silence stretched out, but Emily remained quiet. Wait time was one of her most effective tools as a teacher. Finally, Stephanie sighed and dropped her hands. "Look. I don't know what happened to Jim or why. He was a wonderful man, and things were starting to get serious between us. I want whoever did this to him to be caught and punished." She gulped in air and swiped at her eyes. "But," she continued, "but…I really don't think Helen is behind this either. She's in here all the time. We've even ran some 5Ks together. What possible motive could she have for hurting Jim?"

Emily leaned forward. "That's what we want to find out. We can't find any information from Jim's past older than eleven years ago. How long had you and Jim been dating?"

Stephanie twisted her hands together. "We'd been seeing each other steadily for about six months. We met here at the gym. I was leaving late one night, he offered to walk me to my car, and things progressed from there."

Tad spoke up. "What can you tell us about Jim's life before he moved here?"

"Not much, I'm afraid. Jim never really talked about his past. I know he was close to his brother and that his brother lives in New York. I got the impression that his brother had experienced some terrible loss, but Jim never volunteered any information, and I didn't want to push. As I said, things were progressing between us, but—"

"But?" Tad prompted.

"But the past couple of weeks, Jim was different."

"Different how?" Emily asked.

"I don't know exactly. It was like he was more distracted, on edge. He didn't confide anything, but he did tell me he had a late meeting the night he was killed."

"Do you know who he was meeting?" Emily couldn't keep the eagerness out of her voice. This might be the lead they were looking for.

"No. I didn't even know his meeting was at the school." Stephanie's eyes filled.

Darn it. So much for a lead. Emily stood up and impulsively moved around the desk to give Stephanie a hug. "Again, I'm so sorry for your loss," she said as Stephanie began to sob quietly. "If there is anything either one of us can do for you, please let us know." When Stephanie only nodded, Tad and Emily moved out of the office, shutting the door quietly behind them to give Stephanie some privacy.

"So, what do you think?" Emily asked as they reemerged into the busy gym.

"I think we should try out a few of these machines while we're here on a visitor's pass."

"I meant about Stephanie! And you can forget the machines. You promised me ice cream." Emily gave Tad a push in the direction of the exit.

"All right, all right. Let me apply for a membership first. I like this place."

Emily watched the rain spatter the asphalt, tapping her toe, while Tad dealt, or more like flirted, if you asked her, with the anorexic redhead. Once they were finally in the car, Emily repeated her question.

"I think she's a grieving girlfriend. But she doesn't know anything that really helps us. We found out the brother lives in New York, so maybe we can do some checking there. What're you thinking?" he asked, pulling into their favorite ice cream place.

Emily waited to answer until she had placed her order for a large caramel sundae with extra whipped cream. "I liked Stephanie. But, what if this was a lover's quarrel gone bad? Isn't it usually the boyfriend or girlfriend that the cops look at first? Stephanie is definitely strong enough to have knocked out a guy, even one as big as Jim."

Tad waited until their order was delivered, then, licking chocolate fudge off the end of his spoon, said, "I think you've watched too many *Castle* reruns. We don't have a shred of evidence linking Stephanie to Jim's death."

"Maybe Gabby and I will find some proof tomorrow in Peculiar Bluffs," she said.

Tad didn't respond, and Emily was relived to be spared another lecture. When Tad pulled up in front of her dark home, putting the car in park, he asked, "Do you want me to walk you in?"

Emily shook her head no, but before she could open her door, Tad leaned over and lightly touched her cheek, turning her face toward his. "Please be careful tomorrow" was all he said before he planted a light kiss on her forehead.

Emily nodded mutely, unsure of what to say. And then she was splashing through the rain before Tad could see her flaming cheeks. She noted that Tad didn't budge from the curb until she had locked her door and turned on a light. She couldn't quite contain the glow that spread from her smile to her heart.

CHAPTER EIGHT

———

When Emily's alarm went off at 6:00 a.m. the next morning, she smacked it several times, briefly wondering why she had set her alarm for a Saturday morning, before remembering the trip planned for today. She had less than twenty minutes to throw herself together by the time she actually dragged herself from beneath her warm, snuggly comforter.

When she pulled up to Gabby's at 7:05 a.m., she was patting herself on the back for only being five minutes late. But then she burst out laughing at Gabby sneaking out the back patio doors like a cat burglar. She tiptoed all the way to the car, looking over her shoulder every couple of feet. She slipped into the passenger seat and silently eased the door shut.

"Got the cash?" Emily asked in a conspiratorial whisper, trying to look serious.

Gabby smacked her arm. "Ha. Ha. Just one of the perks of the job of mom. Phoebe slept much better last night, but if she or Abigail knew I was heading somewhere with their Aunt Emily, they would badger me to no end to go with us. This way, no tears, no stress."

"Whatever you say, O Wise One," Emily laughed as she pulled out of the drive.

"And here I come bearing gifts." Gabby sniffed, rummaging in the tote bag she had at her feet. She came out with a thermos and an insulated cup. "Coffee for me and Coke for you. I know how much you love mornings."

"I take back every mean thing I've ever said." Emily slapped one hand over her heart and batted her eyelashes at Gabby.

"Sure you do. But here you go anyway." Emily slurped happily away as she navigated the exit onto the interstate.

Gabby settled back in her seat and inhaled her own favorite beverage of choice. Emily tried not to be jealous of the fact that Gabby, as usual, looked glamorous and put together, the polar opposite of Emily's thrown-together look. Last night, after Emily had called the school in Peculiar Bluffs to set up a meeting with the principal, a Mr. Wells, she had laid out an outfit that she thought looked both professional and friendly. Today, her outfit of trouser jeans and a plum, shawl-collared sweater, with black, stiletto-heeled boots seemed downright dowdy next to Gabby's tailored linen slacks and coral blazer with a coordinating paisley scarf. Emily shrugged off her worries, as it was too late for wardrobe changes, and instead focused on the mission at hand.

"So what did this Mr. Wells have to say? Did he sound surprised to hear about Jim's death?" Gabby asked, shielding her eyes with one hand to better see. The temperature might be hovering around forty degrees, but the sun was a fierce competitor, battling to keep the cold at bay.

"Very," Emily nodded, checking her rearview mirror before changing lanes. "When I described the situation, he said he would be happy to meet with us. Sounds like Jim was a well-loved coach at Peculiar Bluffs too."

"Anything else?" Gabby turned fully in her seat to put her back to the sun.

"He wanted a description of who to be looking out for since we're meeting him on a Saturday."

"What'd you tell him?"

Emily kept her gaze pointed straight ahead. "I told him to expect one gorgeous woman with long, dark, curly hair—and a body to die for, despite having given birth to twins, and…" She paused as Gabby scoffed.

"What? You know it's true." Gabby shrugged and stared straight ahead too. Even when they were in their teens, Gabby had never wanted to draw attention to her looks, but that hadn't stopped the boys from drooling. Emily had always envied Gabby because she was a true stunner, but Gabby's sweetness and huge heart kept that envy from ever turning into jealousy. Now, if Gabby had been tall and well-endowed on top of her beauty, it might have been a different story, but thankfully for their friendship, Gabby was every bit as short and flat-chested as Emily was.

"All right, I might have left that last part off."

Gabby gave her a light punch to the shoulder. "So how did you describe yourself, then?"

"Oh, you know, the usual. I simply told him that I was six feet tall, have legs that won't quit, and generally look like a Victoria's Secret model."

When Gabby's mouth dropped open, Emily tried to act offended but ended up giggling instead. "Okay, I really told him I was short, chubby, and have dark, bobbed hair. Better?"

"No," Gabby grumped, crossing her arms. Emily knew what was coming next. "For the last time, Emily Grace, you are *not* chubby!"

"Okay, okay. Calm down. Let's go with 'not skinny.'"

"If you want to lose a few pounds, you can always start running with me. As I recall, that was one of your New Year's resolutions, right?"

"I was delusional. It was late at night. Or early in the morning. Neither time is good for me. Everyone was making absurd resolutions. I can't be held responsible for what I said during New Year's Eve mania."

Gabby merely raised an eyebrow.

Emily sighed, as if in defeat. "All right. You win. I will start running"—Gabby straightened up and beamed—"if my home is ever on fire or I'm being chased by an axe murderer." Gabby's smile disappeared, and she slouched back down in her seat.

"You're impossible," was her only response.

"Yeah. But you love me anyway. How about some tunes?" Emily knew her lazy ways were forgiven when Gabby started fiddling with the radio.

It was a perfect fall day, and they sang along to the songs they knew, humming or making up words to the ones they didn't. If they hadn't been on such a serious fact-finding mission, the trip would have had all the makings for a perfect girls' day out. Before they knew it, they were passing the city limit sign for Peculiar Bluffs. Emily followed the signs to the main thoroughfare, where the principal had told her the high school was located.

"Oh, I forgot to tell you!" Gabby suddenly exclaimed, making Emily jump. "Sorry. I just remembered. I called Serenity Falls yesterday."

"You did? I figured you might have been too busy with Phoebe being sick and all. What did you find out?"

"Well, I wasn't sure how to play it, but—"

"Wait. How to play what? You were only supposed to be finding out how much a room there cost."

"Yeah, I know. Still, I told them that I had a mother dealing with the early stages of dementia and that my brother and I were looking at Serenity Falls as a suitable place for her."

Emily choked on a large gulp of soda. "You did not!"

"I did," Gabby answered smugly. "I didn't want them to think I was fishing for information. That seemed rude."

"Finding out a nursing home's annual fee is definitely not a fishing expedition. And if your mom knew what you'd done, she'd tan your hide." Maria Moretti, Gabby's mom, might be barely five feet tall, but her spitfire personality was legendarily grand. She was currently in perfect health and celebrating her thirty-fifth anniversary with her husband, Carl, in Rome.

"Oh, I know. That's why I didn't give my name. She would murder me in my sleep…and wow, that was a poor choice of words."

Emily grimaced. "Anyway…"

"The cost for a basic room at Serenity Falls is $72,000 annually. And I don't know about you, but I highly doubt the room Ms. Quinton was in was a basic room."

Emily was too shocked for words. "Seventy-two thousand dollars? No, I don't think that was a basic room. How in the world does Helen afford that?"

They were both silent, thinking of what this information might mean for Helen. Emily felt discouraged by the information, but she prayed they'd discover something useful in their visit with the principal of Peculiar Bluffs High School. A large stone building could be seen coming up on their right. "I think this is it," she told Gabby. The building looked old, yet impressive. She and Gabby got out and stretched their trip-weary legs.

"Check out that football field." Gabby motioned to the professional-looking stadium next to the school. "Hard to see why Coach Layton would have ever left."

"Let's go find out." Emily led the way up the stairs to the double doors. They opened before they could reach them, and a tall, skinny-bordering-on-skeletal man stepped out. "Ms. Taylor?" he asked.

Emily nodded and shook his hand, introducing Gabby next.

"Please, come into my office, and we'll talk. I'm sorry to be meeting you under such sad circumstances. Jim Layton was a great man."

As they made their way down the hall, Gabby whispered in Emily's ear, "I think he's sad we're not supermodels." Emily covered her snort with a cough, moving forward to take the chair Mr. Wells indicated.

He took a seat behind his desk and leaned forward. "I wish I had more that I could tell you. It's so hard to believe that Jim is gone. He was a beloved coach and teacher and led us to back-to-back state championships during the five years he was here. We were sorry to lose him."

"Why did he leave?"

"I was never sure. When Jim came to us from New York, he had excellent teaching references. However, it was clear he needed a fresh start. Apparently, his brother had suffered a great personal loss. He didn't discuss it with anyone, and I didn't push for particulars as he was so highly recommended. I often wondered if he was a witness to something and was trying to escape or hide."

"Can you tell us where in New York he came from?"

"I tried to look up his personnel file, but since he has been gone from the district for more than three years, it's in storage. And it is a Saturday." He gave a *what can you do* shrug.

"We understand," Gabby assured him, trying to cover up their disappointment. "Did he have any disgruntled players or parents, ones who thought their little Bobby or Johnny deserved more playtime or something?"

"No, nothing like that." Mr. Wells sounded confident. "He got along with everyone. He was friendly but never really hung out with the other teachers outside of work. They said he always seemed to have personal business to attend to on the weekends."

"What about a girlfriend?" Emily asked.

"Not that I know of, and I think I'd know. Jim was a regular customer at Elsie's Café, also known as gossip central in this town, so if Jim was seeing someone, it would have been fodder for the gossip mill there. Again, I wish I had more to tell you."

"No, no. We appreciate you meeting us on a Saturday. You've been very helpful." Emily smiled warmly, but she felt distinctly frustrated at the shortness of their visit and the lack of any new information.

"Anything else I can help you girls with?" Mr. Wells stood.

Emily and Gabby shook their heads, and Mr. Wells escorted them out. Back in the car, they both stared out the window. "So what did we learn?"

"This is the second time we've heard of Jim's brother and a loss. That can't be a coincidence. Right?"

"Right," Gabby agreed. "So where to now?"

"Don't know about you, but I'm hungry."

"Elsie's Café?"

"You read my mind." Emily plugged the eatery's name into her GPS, and they headed out.

* * *

The sign outside Elsie's Café proudly proclaimed it served the world's best pie. "My kind of place," Gabby declared as the tiny bell over the door tinkled at their arrival. Emily instantly fell in love with the 1950's diner décor. The booths were covered in a soothing aqua tone, while bright yellow sunflowers in white vases added a cheerful pop of color. They were seated in a booth by the window by a similarly cheery waitress. They both ordered waters and perused the extensive menu. "Man, they have everything here. I think I'll try the double bacon cheeseburger and fries, with more cheese," Gabby decided.

Emily looked at her slim friend over the top of her menu. "Where do you put it?" she asked. Gabby ignored her, so she went back to trying to decide between the Philly cheesesteak and the chicken parm sandwich. By the time the waitress had made her way back to their booth, she had settled on the cheesesteak.

Emily and Gabby reviewed the little Mr. Wells had been able to tell them as they waited on their lunch. It certainly wasn't much, and while they were in agreement that the New York connection was important, they couldn't see how to tie that back to Helen. Helen had been a counselor at Ellington High for more than twenty years. She was practically old enough to be Jim's mother, so it was hard to comprehend where they might have crossed paths outside of school. They were no closer to a solution by the time their food arrived. It lived up to its reputation, and they both relished every bite. Dunking a fry in cheese, Gabby asked, "What if the two aren't related at all?"

"Two what?" Emily asked, caught up in her Philly.

"Jim's murder and Helen's disappearance. What if they're not connected at all?"

Emily swallowed the last bite of her sandwich and stared at her plate as if it were a departing lover. All good things must come to an end, but that didn't mean you had to like it, Emily thought. "I guess that's always a possibility. But think about it. Ellington is not exactly a hotbed of crime. Two major, incidents we'll call them, in one night seems like an improbable coincidence. Factor in that they both worked at the school and the murder occurred there, and the chances of them being unrelated seem even higher."

Gabby nodded. "I think the problem is that if they are related, don't we have to consider that Helen could be guilty and is on the run?"

Emily stirred her water with her straw, creating a whirlpool in her glass. That's exactly how her life felt right now—she was spinning in circles, her world out of sorts. "I guess so. But then we have to circle back to motive. Why would Helen kill Jim? What was their connection?"

Gabby picked up the dessert menu and frowned. "Maybe we should ask to speak to the owner or manager. If Jim spent a lot of time here, maybe he talked to him or her."

"Good point. I'll catch our waitress."

As it turned out, the owner actually was the original Elsie, a skinny, yet busty, redhead who snapped her gum as she approached their table. As she slid into the booth beside Emily, she half expected to hear her say "Kiss my grits." Over truly excellent pie—apple for Emily and strawberry rhubarb for Gabby—they questioned Elsie concerning what she knew about Jim.

Elsie had no idea that Jim had been murdered, and she seemed genuinely upset as she wiped her tears on the edge of the checkered apron she wore. "Who would want to hurt a nice fella like Jim?" she asked them. Emily explained that was what they were hoping to find out.

"He stopped in here nearly every day. He struck me as a man on a mission, always on the alert," Elsie said.

Gabby patted Elsie's hand, as the older woman was still swiping at tears. "Did he ever talk to you about what this mission might be?"

"No," Elsie said haltingly.

"But?" Emily asked, picking up on her hesitation.

"I found it odd that such a nice man, and not a bad-looking one either, if I do say so myself, was always alone. He needed a woman to take care of him. To feed him proper-like." Elsie patted her fire-engine red hair, and Emily hid a smile. Elsie was definitely old enough to be Jim's mother.

"So you never saw him with anyone? No best friend? No girlfriend?" Gabby frowned as she asked. As an inherently social creature, self-chosen solitude was a foreign concept to her.

"Nope. He always came in alone. He had a fondness for my coconut cream pie." Elsie sniffed again and waved over one of the hovering waitresses. "Bring me a slice of that coconut cream pie I just set out." As the waitress hurried away to do her bidding, Elsie turned back to Emily and Gabby. "In tribute to Jim." Emily nodded. She ached for this woman's genuine grief, but she had to find out something that would help Helen.

"Had Jim been acting differently before he left town? Did he ever seem troubled? Talk about any enemies?"

Elsie wiped meringue from the freshly delivered slice of pie off her lip, considering Emily's questions. "Nope. Jim had a kind word for everybody and never complained. He'd get some good-natured ribbing from other regulars when his boys lost a game, but he took that in stride. Like I said, Jim was a nice guy. Everyone liked him."

Emily chewed her lip. So far, the only thing she'd gained from this side trip to Elsie's was another pound or two on her hips thanks to the generous proportions and truly excellent pie. She watched Elsie scrape the last creamy bit off her plate, licking the fork. The waitress Elsie had called over before had returned with a check, and Gabby was reaching for her purse. Elsie stopped her. "This one's on the house," she told them.

"You don't have to do that," Gabby protested.

"But I do. Let me know if you find out anything about why someone would want to hurt poor Jim." Emily assured her they would, and after thanking her for lunch and her time once again, she and Gabby made their way out of the café into the afternoon sunshine.

"So what now?" Gabby asked, slipping on her sunglasses.

"I don't know. Home, I guess." Emily couldn't hide the disappointment in her voice as she turned to unlock the car. She was sliding into the driver's seat when she heard a "yoo-hoo" from behind her. She and Gabby both turned to see Elsie trotting after them, her apron flapping in the breeze.

"Whew." She leaned a hand against the car, catching her breath. "I thought of one thing I did find odd about Jim's behavior before he moved away."

"What?" Emily and Gabby asked in unison.

"Jim rented a little apartment near the school. I knew his landlord, and they were both happy with the arrangement. But a month or so before Jim moved, he was talking about buying a house. He ruffled a few feathers by going to several different realtors rather than sticking with one. But he seemed to have settled on a house. Even told me he'd put in an offer, and then the next thing I hear, he's packed up and moved away."

"Do you know what realtors he talked to or where the house was?" Emily asked.

Elsie shook her head. "No. Jim always kept things close to the vest. Like I said, a man on a mission."

Emily and Gabby thanked her again and watched her hurry back to her customers. "Should we check out the realtor offices?" Gabby asked.

"I don't know what good it would do. Jim never bought the house, and that was five years ago. It's getting late. We'd better head back. The girls will be wondering where you are."

"Yeah, I hate to be gone too late, what with Phoebe's cough yesterday and all."

They stopped to fill up with gas and grab a drink for the road, and then they were on their way home. Gabby called and checked in with Greg, and Phoebe was doing fine. Abigail, however, was now sporting a runny nose and her own cough. "Looks like another long night at my house." Emily looked over at her exhausted-looking friend. It was moments like this that she was grateful not to have the worry of a child. She couldn't imagine the frustration of not being able to "fix" them. But oh, how she one day hoped to have those worries.

"Is there anything I can do to help?"

Gabby gave her a tired smile. "I appreciate it, but no. It'll run its course soon enough. Our first hard freeze will help with the allergies."

"I'm sorry I drug you up here. Wish we had found out more."

"Oh, I don't think it was a waste of time. Let's look at what we did find out. We know that Jim came here from New York and there was some trouble surrounding his brother. Could that information have been discovered by someone in Ellington and been important, or sinister, enough to blackmail him over?"

Emily banged her fist lightly on the steering wheel in frustration. "That's a possibility, but why wait until now? Jim had been at Ellington almost six years."

"And what about what Elsie said about his sudden move when he was looking at buying a house?"

"I know. That's a puzzle to me, as well. I'm pretty sure he was a renter over there on Elm Street back home. I can't imagine what Jim could have in his past that was worth blackmailing him over. He seemed like such a nice, normal guy."

"That's what the neighbors always say about the psychotic killers that have been living next to them for years." Gabby yawned.

"True," Emily admitted. "But Jim was the one who was murdered, not the murderer."

"Yeah, but I think there was something to what Mrs. Quinton said about money. I'm worried she was talking about blackmail money. And that might make Helen a blackmailer, which is the exact opposite of what we believe. This playing Nancy Drew is hard." Gabby reclined her seat slightly. "What do you think, Em? Could we be wrong about Helen?"

"I still believe Helen is innocent. And the longer her disappearance lasts, I'm afraid the authorities will see her absence as her running from guilt. Helen doesn't have a single quality about her that makes me think she could be a blackmailer, let alone a murderer. But Mr. Barnes, on the other hand…he is one I can see blackmailing, or even offing, somebody."

"Offing? Is he related to Jimmy Hoffa? You have some major hatred for this guy, Em, and that is not like you."

"There's just something about him that oozes smarmy. And blackmailing is definitely smarmy. Besides, how else did he afford that new car of his?"

Emily heard a slight snore from the seat beside her. "Gabby?"

"Sorry. Mr. Barnes? I don't know. Family money?" Gabby's eyes drifted closed before she had even finished her sentence.

"Why don't you catch a cat nap? We can talk this over with Greg and Tad once we get home."

"You sure you don't mind?" Gabby asked, even as she reclined her seat further.

"Nope. You need the rest. You're in good hands." At that, Gabby sat up straight.

"You better mean that, Em. I remember vowing never to sleep in a car you were driving after that two-lane passing-on-a-hill stunt you tried back when we were teenagers."

Emily gave her a dry stare. "That was more than ten years ago, Gabby. But suit yourself."

"I didn't mean to insult you, but you have to admit that your driving record is not exactly stellar." Emily only gave a noncommittal shrug, so Gabby continued. "I have two kiddos who need me well and whole. Just saying."

"Just saying," Emily mimicked, but no one heard her. Gabby was already fast asleep.

CHAPTER NINE

———

    Red and gold streaked across the twilight-blue sky as Emily hummed along to the radio that was playing quietly in accompaniment to Gabby's snores. Thoughts and facts about Jim's murder rained down in her mind like a ticker-tape parade. First and foremost was the question of where Helen could be. Her absence seemed to solidify her guilt, but Emily still didn't believe she was capable of committing a crime. Was she in trouble? How could they find her? Maybe Tad was right. Perhaps it would be better to leave this to the authorities and not get involved. What did she know about locating a missing person? Or solving a murder, for that matter? Yet even as she questioned her involvement, Emily knew that her need to protect those who mattered to her would never allow her to let this matter drop. Besides, what could asking a few questions hurt? There wasn't any harm in that.

    The first blinding flash of headlights surprised her. The sky was a deep navy-blue now, and the glare of the lights behind her caused her vision to blur with dancing spots of white. This was a deserted stretch of road. Only a few farms were scattered over the next twenty or so miles. Traffic was typically light, and this evening was no exception. The person behind her had ample room to pass. To reinforce that point, Emily tapped her brakes. The headlights stayed squarely in her rearview mirror. Always prone to road rage, Emily's first thought was to have it out with the idiot behind her. She pressed down on her brakes again, prepared to pull over on the shoulder. The headlights started to pass her, and Emily determined to get this jerk's license plate. Before she was completely off the highway, however, the vehicle, which looked to be a dark-colored SUV, slammed into the back door of her PT, right behind her seat. Emily's tires bit into the gravel on the side of the road, seeking traction, while Emily wrestled with the steering wheel.

Gabby rocketed upright, eyes wild. "What's going on? Emily, I told you to be careful!"

She didn't have time to answer or defend herself as the vehicle that had rammed into her backed off, and she was able to slow her car enough to ease back into her lane. She reached for her phone in the console and tossed it at Gabby. "Call the police," she instructed, willing her voice to remain calm as the headlights once again loomed in her rearview mirror.

Gabby made no move to grab the phone, still disoriented from sleep. "What's going on?" she asked again.

The impact of the vehicle ramming them from behind had both of them straining against their locked seat belts. "This idiot is trying to run us off the road!" Emily gasped as she mashed down the accelerator, trying to put some distance between them and the maniacal SUV behind them.

As the speedometer edged toward eighty, Gabby managed to get hold of the phone. "Where are we?" she asked frantically, now fully awake and aware of the true danger they were in.

"About an hour outside Ellington," Emily said through gritted teeth. Topping the rise of a hill, Emily felt her tires temporarily lose contact with the pavement due to the speed at which they were now moving. "The double S curves around the Wiley farm are up ahead. I can't take those at ninety miles an hour."

Gabby let out a sob. "Pull over, Emily. Please."

"I can't," Emily told her. "There's no shoulder here." And there wasn't—only the steep decline to flatter ground far below. "Call the police. Now."

Gabby's fingers trembled as she fought to dial the number. Sweat poured down Emily's back as she flicked glances at her rearview mirror. The headlights were swallowing them up in their glare once again. Emily tried to press the accelerator even further down, but her PT was already giving it all she had. The SUV slammed into the back door again, and the sound of rending metal tore through the stillness of the night. Before Emily could even attempt any evasive maneuver, the SUV barreled into them again, finally forcing them off the road. Emily fought for control, trying to keep them upright. The decline was too steep, however, and the PT tilted up on its right side before slamming back to the ground. Despite her repeated attempts to stomp on the brakes, the vehicle only gained momentum as it skidded down the steep hill. There was no use for her to attempt to steer at this point, even though her hands remained locked on the steering wheel. She could hear Gabby shrieking beside her and felt her own eyes overflow with tears. The sounds of brush and tree limbs scraping down both sides of her vehicle sounded like nails on a chalkboard, but at least the brush slowed their momentum. Emily could only pray the tree limbs would bring the vehicle to a complete stop as her brakes were useless at this point. But then she saw the tree directly in front of them. She only had time to throw her body in Gabby's direction, trying to shield her, while covering her own face with her arms. The crash jarred every bone in her body. Her vision swam red…and then there was nothing but blackness.

* * *

Her alarm was going off again. Hadn't she hit snooze? The alarm continued to blare. How late was it? The sun was shining directly in her eyes. Only it wasn't her alarm. And it wasn't the sun. Emily was flat on her back, with a doctor shining a light in her eyes. The noise was actually the organized chaos of a bustling ER. Obviously, she was in a hospital. But why? She tried to push herself up to ask, but her arm exploded in flames. At least that's what her muddled brain told her. The doctor mercifully put away the light. Too confused to even form questions, Emily felt tears dripping down into her ears. A kind voice and a gentle hand appeared. The hand wiped at her tears, and the voice asked her if she knew where she was.

"It looks like a hospital. But my arm is on fire, and…I don't know why." Emily realized her voice was hoarse and whiny. She cleared her throat. "What happened?" Her question still came out sounding tiny and scared, but then, she reasoned, she felt tiny and scared. She had never liked hospitals, and thankfully, she'd never had to stay in one. She prayed that lucky streak wasn't about to end.

"You had an accident. A man found you and called the ambulance. The ambulance brought you here."

"An accident? Gabby! Where's Gabby?"

"Your friend is being treated in a separate room. She'll be fine. As will you. But the reason you feel like your arm is on fire is because you have a compound fracture. You'll be going into surgery soon. Is there anyone I can call for you?"

And then she remembered. The trip to Peculiar Bluffs. The car trying to run them off the road. The tree. "You're sure Gabby's okay?" she asked instead.

"She has a mild concussion, but she will be right as rain in no time." Gentle and sincere brown eyes looked directly into hers. "I promise."

Emily sobbed out a breath of relief, and a few more tears pooled in her ears. "I don't want to worry my parents. Could you call my friend Tad?" She recited his number and then closed her eyes, trying to come to grips with their situation. They had no transportation, their phones were probably lost, and they were in the hospital. All of that would sound very scary to her parents. But Tad would be calm and level headed. He would tell Greg and make any necessary arrangements. At the thought of Greg and the twins, her ears turned into small pools. Never in her wildest imagination did she think that going to Peculiar Bluffs would put Gabby in any danger.

She must have drifted off from the combined effects of pain and exhaustion, because the next thing she knew, the gentle voice and hands were back, and she was being wheeled into a surgical room. "I called your friend Tad. He'll be here when you wake up. He said to tell you he would take care of everything and not to worry." The pain in Emily's arm was stealing her breath, but she managed to nod weakly. The cool rush of anesthesia brought a welcome return to the darkness.

* * *

This time the light that woke her was not so blinding. Emily cautiously looked around. She was in a hospital bed, a low light burning. A dark head was bent, resting on the edge of her bed. She was ridiculously glad to see Tad, a familiar presence in this nightmare world that she had entered the moment those headlights flashed in her rearview mirror. Emily tried to raise her arm to pat those comforting, disheveled curls, but her arm didn't budge. It was like trying to lift an anvil. She checked out the cast keeping her right arm bent at the elbow. Well, that would certainly take some getting used to. She tried lifting her left arm instead and awkwardly patted the top of Tad's head. He immediately jerked to attention. "What's wrong? Do you hurt? Do I need to call the nurse?"

"I think my brain is too overwhelmed for that many questions, but let me try. I'm glad to see you. I've never been more terrified in my life. I don't hurt too badly right now, but I'm sure I will later. And yes, you need to call a nurse."

"I can help you get out of bed if you need to, um, you know…" Tad gestured toward the bathroom door. "I'll call the nurse," he finished.

"It's not that," Emily told him. "I want out of this bed permanently. I want to go to Gabby. Where is she? How is she?" And now the true horror of what could have happened to her best friend hit her like an avalanche so that she couldn't stop the slide into tears. They weren't pretty tears, either. They were red-eye-inducing, snot-producing, gut-wrenching, sobbing tears. Without a word, Tad crawled up on the bed on her good side and wrapped his arms around her. Emily cried into his soft flannel shirt until she was sure she was dehydrated. Shifting a little, but not removing her cheek from the warm comfort of his chest, she whispered, "Sorry."

Tad gently lifted her chin so that he could look her in the eye. "I think that was inevitable. I'm glad I was here when it hit. Pit, you're going to be okay. And Gabby too. They're keeping her overnight for observation, but she only has a mild concussion."

Emily tried to sit up. "*Only* a mild concussion? She is in the hospital because of me, Tad!"

"Did you run yourself off the road?" Tad asked reasonably.

"How did you know what happened?" she asked him.

"You did some babbling to the nurse who first treated you. Gabby did too. We pieced together that much of the story. The details can wait until you and Gabby are feeling better."

Emily said, "Call the nurse, Tad. I either go to Gabby's room where I can see her for myself, or I will check myself out against medical advice."

Tad pushed at his hair. His eyes briefly closed before he looked down at her once again. "This is going to be one of those things I can't talk you out of, isn't it?"

Emily simply nodded. Tad pushed the button for the nurse, then shifted off the bed and back into the chair he had occupied when she awoke. She missed his strong, warm body next to her. Alone in the bed, she felt swallowed by the white sheets, adrift on a sea of the unfamiliar and frightening.

A woman in crisp blue scrubs marched through the door, her hair pulled back in a severe ponytail. "You called for a nurse?" she asked.

Emily faltered at her stern voice but tried to match her tone for tone. "I want to be released from this bed. I don't plan on leaving the hospital, but I will not stay here. I will be in Gabby Spencer's room."

"I'm afraid that isn't an option, Ms. Taylor. The doctor wants you under observation, as well."

Emily struggled into a sitting position, swinging her legs over the side of the bed. Tad rushed to help her. "I'll be checking out then," Emily informed the dispassionate face.

"Stay here. I'll see what I can do." The nurse turned sharply on the heel of her rubber clogs without a backward glance. Emily slumped against the pillows.

"You sure about this?" Tad asked quietly, propping her up a little more. Emily only had the strength to nod once.

The nurse returned and began unhooking Emily from her various monitors. She didn't say a word, but her set jaw and haughty nose-in-the-air expression spoke volumes. When she handed Emily a stack of release papers to sign, Emily gave Tad a *help me* look and indicated her incapacitated right hand. He held up the forms so she could manage a scrawl with her left.

"Your friend is in Room 310," the nurse informed them in a monotone, scowling over Emily's illegible scrawl.

"Friendly," Emily muttered under her breath, but her sarcastic bravado vanished when she managed to gain her own two feet. The room swam and swirled in a psychedelic haze. She blindly groped for something to hold on to, and then Tad's strong, steady hands were there.

"Easy, Pit," he murmured. "How do you feel?"

"Like I've been in a car wreck," Emily answered. She tried to laugh but humiliated herself by crying instead.

"Let's go see Gabby" was all Tad said. But he kept a supporting hand around her waist as they left the room.

* * *

The long stretch of hallway to Gabby's room might as well have been a jungle trek as exhausted as Emily felt on their arrival. Her body was screaming at her for its multiple scrapes and bruises, but it was the sight of Gabby in her hospital bed that brought Emily up short.

Gabby's dark curls were brushed back, revealing the purpling bruise running across her temple and spreading down the right side of her face. Greg's back was to them, and he was talking quietly on the phone. Emily clutched Tad's arm harder as Greg turned and spotted them in the doorway. Emily's mind raced as he said his good-byes and hung up the phone. Then everything she'd planned to say was forgotten as she stumbled to him and sobbed, "I'm sorry. I'm so, so sorry." Those were the only words she could manage.

Greg, who had always been like a brother to her, gently pulled her back with his hands on her shoulders. "Em, you have nothing to be sorry for, because this was Not. Your. Fault."

"But Gabby…" Emily faltered, gesturing toward the still form of her friend.

"Gabby is going to be fine. They're finally letting her rest now. Looks like you need to do the same."

"Yes, she does." This nurse had corkscrew curls and freckles. The opening lines of "The Sun Will Come out Tomorrow" ran through Emily's mind. "I know you've signed your discharge papers, but the doctor has prescribed you a pain pill, if you want it." She smiled at Emily and tilted her head, waiting for her response.

"That's something I won't argue with." Emily was starting to feel just how badly her arm throbbed. The nurse beamed at her as if she'd won a spelling bee as she handed her the little white paper cup. Emily managed to swallow the pill despite the lump of guilt and regret constricting her throat. Tad pulled up a chair next to Gabby's bed, and Emily wearily eased into it. She held Gabby's limp hand in her own, grateful it was warm despite her pale cheeks. She turned to Tad. "Thank you for everything. You should go home and get some rest." When he nodded, Emily lowered her head to the side of Gabby's bed, much the same way Tad had done at hers earlier. She just needed to rest her eyes for a moment.

* * *

A light tap on her shoulder roused her from sleep. Emily jerked up, wiping drool from her chin. A quick glance showed her that Gabby was still resting peacefully, but dawn now painted its brilliant colors across the canvas of the sky. The crick in her neck told her she had been asleep for several hours. As she got gingerly to her feet, she wasn't sure which weighed more heavily on her—her guilt or her cast-encased arm. When she turned to see who had woken her, the sight of her parents tipped the scales in favor of guilt. Still, she was thankful for the sling that helped support her arm.

Emily stepped out into the hallway with her mom and dad. The grays, whites, and institutional greens of the hospital contrasted sharply with the pink, orange, and gold of the sunrise she had glimpsed out the window. The only color in the hallway came from her mom's red, swollen eyes and her blindingly bright-fuchsia top. She raced forward to hug Emily, careful to avoid her arm. Her dad was next, and when Emily felt him tremble, she leaked a few more tears.

"We were so worried. Why didn't you call?" Her mom was wiping at her eyes again.

"Precisely because I didn't *want* to worry you." Emily patted her mom's back and glared daggers at Tad, who she saw was lurking at the end of the hallway. The coward.

"We thought you might need backup. We're so thankful Tad called us." Her dad sounded so serious, Emily almost laughed.

"I'm sure Greg's more upset with me than he's letting on, but I don't think I'll require backup."

Her mom shook her head at Emily's words and pointed toward the other end of the hallway. Detective Gangly-Arms was eating up the scarred linoleum with his long strides. He stopped in front of their assembled group, and without preamble, said, "You are two extremely lucky ladies. I've seen the accident site, and it's a wonder you didn't roll your vehicle."

Emily nodded. "Yes, Detective. I'm very thankful. But why are you here exactly? Isn't this a little outside your jurisdiction?"

Tad stepped forward. "I called him."

Emily brushed at her matted hair. It was too early in the morning to play twenty questions. She stared silently at both Tad and the detective. Before either could speak, Greg called out, "She's awake!"

Emily rushed to Gabby's bedside, weak with relief to see some color back in her friend's cheeks. "Hey," Gabby croaked.

"Hey back," Emily whispered. She leaned over and gently hugged her best friend in all the world. "I'm so sorry," she sobbed. "That's all I know to say, and it's not enough."

"Stop that right now," Gabby ordered, sounding more like her old self. "Greg"—she turned to her husband—"help me sit up, will you?" Greg propped some more pillows behind her, then she continued, once again addressing Emily. "For once, your terrible driving was not your fault. That vehicle ran us off the road!" Gabby looked absolutely outraged.

"And that's why I'm here," Detective Gangly-Arms spoke up. Gabby took his presence in her hospital room in stride and introduced herself.

"Care to tell me what you two were doing up in Peculiar Bluffs?" he asked, pulling out his notebook.

"Why?" Emily countered.

"Come off it, Em. This is serious." Tad stepped forward, her parents on his heels. "You know as well as we do that this wasn't some random accident. Someone knows you're digging into Layton's past, and they're not happy about it." Tad looked furious, but Emily didn't know what to say. She wasn't even sure who he was actually furious with.

"Mr. Higginbotham is right. Now I'll ask you again, what were you two doing up in Peculiar Bluffs?"

"Talking to Jim Layton's old principal. Trying to find out where he was before coming to Iowa," Gabby answered.

"And what did you find out?" the detective inquired, taking notes.

"Nothing, besides he came from New York and had a brother who suffered some kind of loss." Emily answered this time but then couldn't help adding, "But I'm sure you already knew that."

Detective Gangly-Arms ignored her, instead asking, "What can you tell me about the vehicle that ran you off the road?"

"It was a dark color—maybe black, maybe dark blue. It was some kind of SUV, but that's really all I can tell you. It was full dark by then, and their headlights pretty much blinded us."

Gabby nodded her agreement. "I had fallen asleep, and then the next thing I know, we're being rammed by some psycho. I was trying to call the police. I'm not sure I ever got that done, though," she added thoughtfully.

"No," the detective told her. "No 9-1-1 call was received. A man who farms in this area heard the crash and called for help."

"We need to get his name," Emily's mom spoke up. "I want to thank him."

The detective nodded. "I'll get that to you." He turned back to Emily. "You two should be thanking your lucky stars, you know that? Your vehicle was completely totaled."

Emily gulped. That stung. But compared to their lives, the PT's loss was inconsequential.

"You've been very helpful," the detective added as a doctor bustled in to check on Gabby.

Emily followed Gangly-Arms into the hallway. "What exactly do you mean by 'helpful?'" she asked.

"We've been searching for Ms. Burning's car since the night she disappeared. You do know what she drives?" Emily's heart sank as she pictured Helen's navy-blue Tahoe. Detective Gangly-Arms continued, "The vehicle that ran you off the road has to have extensive damage. Hopefully, we'll get lucky and hear from a repair shop."

"You know Helen's innocent." Emily craned her neck to look straight into his eyes.

"All I know, Ms. Taylor, is that I'm performing an investigation. One I expect you will stay out of from now on. Understood?" Emily stared at the floor, battling her anger. "I'm sure you don't want to see anyone else you care about get hurt," the detective added.

"Of course not," Emily snapped, turning and bumping into Tad.

"He's right, you know," Tad said softly as they watched the detective disappear down the hallway.

Again, Emily was silent. Naturally, she wanted those she loved safe. But 'ole Gangly-Arms was *not* right. Emily was more convinced than ever that Helen was innocent and possibly in danger. Helen knew Emily's vehicle. Helen would never hurt her or anyone else.

"They're letting Gabby go," Tad cut into her thoughts. "Let's get Nancy Drew and her sidekick home so they can rest, recover, and retire their investigative hats."

Emily followed Tad back into the hospital room. He could think what he wanted, but she knew she had implicated Helen by telling the detective that the vehicle that had run them off the road was a dark SUV. Whoever had totaled her PT and hurt Gabby was going to pay. Emily would make sure of it. And when she did, Helen's innocence would be proven once and for all.

CHAPTER TEN

———

Climbing into the back seat of her parents' car, Emily felt like she was ten years old again. Her mom, just like when Emily would have to come home early because she had gotten sick at school, had filled the car with her favorite pillows and blankets. Her mom had also had to help her into the change of clothes she had brought with her. Emily had been sure she would have to leave the hospital in one of their unsightly gowns. When one of the nurses had brought her the clothes she was wearing in the accident, she hadn't given them a second glance before tossing them in the nearest trash can.

Now safely on her way home, Emily deeply regretted that she had worried her parents, but she did not regret taking action to help Helen. She wasn't sure if she should brace for a lecture, defend herself, or both, so she decided to feign sleep. That wasn't hard since she was so tired, her hair hurt. Her dad's voice broke the uneasy silence, hanging like a curtain between them, before she could escape into dreamland. "So, kiddo, what did you and Gabby find out?"

Emily wiped a tear of relief from her cheek before she answered. Leave it to her dad to put her at ease. Her mom remained staring straight ahead, but Emily leaned forward and began telling them all they had discovered while in Peculiar Bluffs. Her dad nodded along as she described her and Gabby's talk with Mr. Wells. He seemed interested in the whole "brother in New York" angle, but her mom's back remained straightjacket stiff, and her eyes never left the road until Emily mentioned the cost of living at Serenity Falls.

"Seventy-two thousand dollars?" she exclaimed, whipping around in her seat to stare at Emily. "That's outrageous! How could Helen afford that?" Emily met her dad's eyes in the rearview mirror, but neither one of them spoke a word. Their silence strained against their belief that Helen was innocent.

To lighten the mood, she joked, "Guess you and dad will have to live next door or something if you need care in your old age." The minute the words left her mouth, Emily regretted them. If her parents were able to live next door, then Helen would not have been found. No words could soothe over the hurt, frustration, and worry that permeated every inch of the car, so Emily leaned her head back and cradled her aching arm. This time she didn't have to pretend to be asleep. Exhaustion won. She slept soundly until she heard her parents' whispered arguing. She took a bleary look out the window. They had reached the city limits of Ellington.

"What's up, Doc?" she asked. Her parents both shot her guilty looks in the rearview mirror. An "uh-oh" feeling sprouted in her stomach.

"I think that with all you've been through and the fact that someone ran you off the road, you should stay with us for a while," her mom said defiantly, her gaze challenging, as she turned in her seat to look at Emily.

Her dad's teacher voice overrode any complaints Emily might have made. He had a way of commanding attention without ever raising his voice. It was one of Emily's goals to master that voice, but at the moment, it grated. "I was telling your mom that I thought you might feel better in your own home, surrounded by your own things." Emily began to nod vehemently, but her dad continued. "So your mom wants to stay with you."

"Oh, Mom, I appreciate your concern, I really do, but I'll be fine. Really." All Emily wanted was the comfort of her own place and peace and quiet in which to think.

"You could be in danger," her mother protested. Emily looked at her dad. They both knew she was perfectly capable of taking care of herself. Emily had practically grown up on the shooting range with her dad.

"I can protect myself in my own home. You know that, Mom. And if I need anything at all, I'll call you. I promise."

Her mom sniffed. "Do you also promise not to do any more digging around in all this murder stuff? I mean, I love Helen, but you're my daughter. I couldn't live without you, Em." Now they were both sniffling. Emily promised, but she crossed her fingers behind her back, so it didn't *really* count.

Once her mom and dad had her settled on her couch with the remotes, her phone—miraculously recovered from the scene of the "accident"— and a bottle of water and some crackers and cheese, Emily finally managed to convince them to go home. The minute they left, she was up and pacing. There were too many thoughts in her head to sit still. She decided a hot shower would help her relax and clear her mind, but once the water was running, she suddenly felt exposed. The silence she had craved was now deafening. Before she stepped into the shower, she dug around in the bottom of her underwear drawer for her .38 Special, which she placed on the toilet lid. That gave her a modicum of reassurance, but unfortunately, her shower still was not relaxing as she spent the next fifteen minutes performing every kind of contortion imaginable trying to get clean but keep her cast dry. By the time she turned off the water, the floor was soaking wet, and she felt as sore as the one—and only—time Gabby had dragged her to a yoga class. She fumbled through toweling herself off and managed to pull on a pair of sweatpants. Even her baggiest shirt ended up with a tear from trying to position it over her cast. Instead of being more relaxed, she was now miserable, sore, and thirsty. She stalked her way to the refrigerator, taking out her frustrations by yelling her head off. No one was around to hear her, so why not?

She was halfway down the hall and in midscream when her doorbell rang. Emily froze. Her heart dropped into her stomach and then rebounded into her throat, where its continued dribbling had her gasping for air. She raced to the bathroom to retrieve her gun, then hovered in the doorway, thanking God that she was left eye dominant, even though she was a right-hander. Despite her nerves, she was proud to see that the hand holding her gun was rock steady.

The doorbell pealed again, and Emily toyed with the idea of calling the police. The problem with that plan was she had left her phone on the couch when she went to take a shower.

The couch was in plain sight of the front windows and therefore also to whoever was at the front door. *Why hadn't she closed the blinds?* She wondered this as the doorbell rang insistently yet again. Whoever was out there was going to wear that thing out. Maybe she should replace it with chimes. That ring was awfully annoying. Wait—was she actually considering doorbell choices at a time like this? Apparently she was, so she must not be as afraid as her bouncing heart told her she was. Because, now that she thought about it, what axe murderer rang the doorbell before slitting your throat? She headed for the door, but not before shoving her gun in the waistband of her sweats where she could feel its reassuring presence against the small of her back. Just in case.

This time the ringing of the doorbell was accompanied by the banging of fists and a frantic voice. "Emily?" the voice bellowed. She hurried to undo the locks and throw the door open for a wild-eyed Tad. "What's wrong?" they both said at the same time.

"You first," Emily gestured.

"When you didn't answer, I thought something might have happened. Like you fell, or someone was in there with you, someone who wanted to hurt you," Tad panted, pushing her behind him in what she assumed he thought of as a protective gesture, scanning her living room for any evildoers. "What took you so long to answer the door?"

Emily gave a tiny shrug. "I thought you might be an axe murderer."

"Ringing the doorbell?"

"It's been a long weekend" was all Emily could come up with. She pushed the front door shut and went to collapse on the sofa. "Ouch," she muttered as soon as she sank into the cushions.

Tad was immediately at her side. "What is it? Is it your arm? What can I do?"

Emily smiled weakly. "Thanks, but I got this." She pulled the .38 Special out of her waistband, checked the safety, and then laid it on the coffee table in front of them.

"Oh." Tad looked from the gun to her and back again. "Forgot you were Annie Oakley. Guess you got things covered on the protection front."

"Yeah, I'm good. Just tired." What she really was, was thirsty, but she had never made it as far as the refrigerator. As if reading her mind, Tad opened the door, grabbed some things off her porch, and locked them in. He handed Emily a large white cup with a red straw, then turned to draw the blinds.

"It's like you read my mind. I could kiss you." Emily took a giant swig of soda, then felt her cheeks blaze with embarrassment. When would she learn to think before she opened her mouth?

"Then I can't wait to see what you'll give me for this." Tad dangled a white takeout bag in front of her nose.

"You didn't," she said.

"I did," Tad replied, pulling out crispy fried chicken and fluffy, golden biscuits. "I made sure to ask for all legs. Thought they would be easier to eat one-handed."

Emily felt tears prick her eyes. She had been telling the truth. It *had* been a long weekend, she *was* tired, and she *had* thought she wanted to be alone. But it was nice to have someone know her well enough to bring her favorite things. She had already taken a bite of warm, buttery biscuit before she saw the duffel bag at Tad's feet. Her heart slam-dunked its way back to her stomach. She motioned to the bag. "What's that for? Did my parents send you over to kidnap me and take me to their house? Because let me tell you, Tad, I'm not going anywhere."

"Good. I'm not either." With that proclamation, Tad flopped down beside her and dug into his own supper.

Emily cleared her throat of suddenly dry biscuit crumbs. "Excuse me?"

"Look, don't be unreasonable about this, Pit. Your parents are worried. Your friends are worried. I had your parents take Duke for a while, and I'm going to crash here on your couch in case you need anything." He stared at her in much the same way her mom had earlier, as if defying her to tell him no. She wanted to, but she was too tired for the whole righteous indignation act. Maybe after a chicken leg. And another biscuit. Or two. Emily shrugged in his direction and said simply, "Thanks."

Tad looked supremely proud of himself as he picked up the remote and picked out a selection of *Castle* reruns from her

DVR. The television show was number one on both of their lists, so they settled in for some good food and some good TV. It was almost like having Gabby over, except Tad was male. Oh, and she never had the urge to cuddle up to Gabby. Trying to push that inappropriate thought from her mind, she said, "I wish we could examine all the clues, interview all the suspects, and figure out what happened to Jim in the next hour like Beckett and Castle do."

"Only this is real life, not television, and your mom said you promised to stay out of this from now on. Right?"

Emily only gave him a noncommittal shrug, not in the mood for an argument. She could barely hold her eyes open as it was. Saying nothing, Tad reached over and cupped her cheek with his hand, his thumb brushing gently at the corner of her mouth. Emily felt herself swaying toward him, feeling like she was in a dream, a dream where she was the princess about to be kissed by Prince Charming. Seeing the glazed look in her eyes, Tad jerked his hand away. "Crumb," he explained. Emily nodded, trying not to feel disappointed.

"Let me get your pain pills. Your mom had your prescription filled," Tad said, hopping up from the couch like a jack-in-the-box. Emily stood slowly, but still the room swayed. The pain, the lack of sleep, and the worry were finally taking their toll. She submitted without a word when Tad led her to her bedroom and tucked her in. She might have been sad to see him leave the room, but knowing he was right outside her door, she rolled over on her left side, propped her heavy, aching right arm on a pillow, and fell into a sound sleep. Analyzing her feelings about Tad would have to wait.

* * *

Emily woke with a dull throb in her arm and a faint smile on her lips. She had been having the most wonderful dream. Tad was looking into her eyes, leaning in to kiss her, and then…She couldn't remember the rest. Strange, she normally remembered most of her dreams. And she didn't normally wake in such a good mood. Turning toward the bedside clock, she let out a yelp—it was 9:45 a.m. She was more than two hours late for school! And Tad!—they must have forgotten to set an alarm. Why hadn't the school called by now? Throwing back the covers, she hurried into the living room, only to see the couch empty, a blanket folded neatly at one end. On closer inspection, she saw a piece of paper on the blanket. She skimmed it quickly. Apparently, Tad had called in for her, explaining the situation. He also promised to be back after school. The note was signed with a quick dash and a *T*. Emily stood for a moment with the note in her hand, unsure of whether to be grateful for Tad's thoughtfulness or irritated by his presumptuousness. Deciding that being grateful would make her the bigger person, Emily pushed open the blinds to let in the sun, then called to check on Gabby.

Greg answered on the first ring and explained to Emily, in hushed tones, that Gabby was still sleeping. She had been pretty woozy from the pain pills still last night. Emily apologized again, but Greg brushed her off, asking how she was doing instead. Emily knew that Greg loved her like a sister, but she also knew he had to be irritated at her that Gabby had been hurt on her watch. As she hung up, the guilt threatened to overwhelm her. Needing an outlet, she headed for her journal, then remembered she couldn't write without the use of her right hand. She backtracked and grabbed her laptop off her desk, settling onto the couch with it. It was still awkward to type one-handed, but desperate times called for desperate measures.

After pouring her heart out concerning her frustrations and guilt, she began to muse about possible suspects in both Jim's murder and their wreck. Emily felt much more empowered dwelling on justice rather than on self-pity. Tapping furiously away at her keyboard, she came up with the following list that she read back to herself:

1. Helen—would never have believed her capable of violence, but did she need money? Was she desperate enough to blackmail someone for money? Was she the one meeting Jim at the school that night? She would have access. If the police were right, could she have run them off the road? She knew Emily's vehicle. Would she risk killing them to end their nosing around? Helen's mother was her top priority, but still,

I have always considered Helen not only a colleague and a friend of my mother's, but one of my own friends, as well. Ugh. Depressing to consider, but evidence dictates that Helen would have had a motive=money, opportunity=access to the school at all hours, and means=?? Helen was a strong, fit woman, but would she have been able to overpower Jim in a struggle? 2. Stephanie—the girlfriend/boyfriend is usually the most likely suspect. She doesn't appear to know much about Jim's past. Could she have been suspicious of him seeing someone else? Could she have followed him to his meeting and hit him over the head? She said Jim had been acting strangely. Could she have found something out that made her afraid of Jim, so afraid that she would kill him? As a personal trainer, she was definitely strong enough to knock Jim down with a blow to the back of the head. She and Jim had to have been close to the same height. She said she didn't know where he was going that night, but she could easily have followed him and slipped into the school before the doors locked. 3. Mr. Barnes—the sneaky rat could be capable of any type of crime. Might be prejudiced, but still...he and Jim never did get along. And how did he get the money for that expensive new toy of his? By blackmailing Jim? What secret could he have held over Jim for money? Would he kill Jim to hide his blackmailing attempts if Jim refused to pay and threatened to turn him in? He would have easy access to the school at night, as well. He practically lived there anyway. Granted, he was a scrawny man, but he was wiry and quick. Most despicable rodents normally were. Please let it be him... 4. Unknown man at the memorial service—who was he? Why did he appear to be sneaking away from the crowd? Could he be someone from Jim's past? Why did he look so familiar? [That was driving her crazy. She was sure she had seen him somewhere before, but where?] *Why would he be at the memorial service? He*

had to have some connection to Jim, yet he didn't
appear to want to talk to any of Jim's friends or
coworkers. What did he drive? Where was he now?

Emily paced the floor. She wished Gabby was awake so she could talk things over with her. She knew that her own personal dislike of Barnes was pushing her to consider him the most likely suspect, but either way, it couldn't hurt to do some checking up on him. Resolved, Emily grabbed a fresh soda and settled back down with her laptop for some armchair detecting. She began by googling Richard Barnes. Thousands of hits turned up, but Emily had no idea how to narrow the search. She couldn't remember how long Mr. Barnes had been at Ellington High or where he came from before that. She scrolled through screens and screens of articles, clicking and scanning each one. Her eyes were burning, and she was ready to call it quits, when a small article from a newspaper in Arkansas caught her eye. A Mr. Richard Barnes had been fired from his job as a chemistry teacher at a small school in the southern part of Arkansas. Despite the fact that he was tenured, the allegations against him led to his dismissal. Emily gaped at the screen, her eyes hungrily devouring the short explanation of the charges against the teacher for being involved in inappropriate conduct with a student. Then she let out a small groan when she read the final sentence—"The charges against Mr. Richard Barnes were dropped due to insufficient evidence. Despite the dismissal of charges, Mr. Barnes has declined to return to his former position."

"I bet," Emily muttered. No one accused of such a thing would want to remain in the same job. She scanned for a date. The article had been published twelve years ago. She wasn't positive, but she thought Mr. Barnes had not been at Ellington much longer than that. One person would know for sure, though. Snatching up her phone, Emily placed a call to her dad. Waiting for him to pick up, she did a little wiggle dance in place on the couch. Finally, she had hard proof to back up her claim that Barnes was one creepy dude.

"How's my favorite girl?" Emily smiled at the warmth in her dad's voice, but she wasn't going to let him off the hook that easily.

"Well, apparently I'm on house arrest now that Tad's calling the shots." She tried to sound more annoyed than she really was.

"You see, about that, I knew that if your mom had her way, you wouldn't have a moment's peace. And I trust Tad, and…well, I worry about you."

Emily softened. She knew her dad truly had her best interests at heart, and as much as she loved her mom, if she came to stay with her, Emily knew they would drive each other crazy within twenty-four hours. Her apartment wasn't big enough for the two of them. "I know, Dad. Thanks, really. I just hate feeling like a victim, you know?"

"I do. And you're not. You're stronger than this." The encouraging, no-nonsense teacher voice that her dad had used in the classroom had its desired effect.

Emily's shoulders snapped to attention, and she got to the point of her call. She wasn't a victim. She was going to figure out what happened to Jim and bring Helen home. "Dad, I was actually calling to ask you some questions about Mr. Barnes."

"Ah, your favorite coworker. What's up?" Emily winced at her dad's words. Apparently her dislike of Barnes was not as well-concealed as she had hoped.

"I did a Google search on him and came up with an interesting article. It would seem that Mr. Barnes was fired from his last job because—"

"Because," her dad interrupted, "he was accused of inappropriate conduct with a student."

"Yeah. Exactly." Emily was surprised that her dad knew about Barnes's indiscretion. She hadn't thought this would be the kind of information he would share with others. "I know that Principal Matthews would never let someone teach at Ellington that he thought was unfit, but…the evidence seems to speak for itself."

"Not really. You see, the allegations were dropped because it was discovered that the claims were bogus. An honor student was upset with the grade she received in chemistry. It ruined her GPA and prevented her from getting some scholarship she had her heart set on. To get back at him, she accused Barnes of inappropriate conduct. I agree that Barnes is an acquired taste, Em, but I don't think he's dangerous."

"I guess." Emily couldn't hide her disappointment.

"Don't sound so thrilled." Her dad laughed. "Besides, you promised to leave this alone. No more poking your nose into other people's business. Believe it or not, the police can handle this without your and Gabby's help."

"I know." She felt a twinge of guilt for her still-crossed fingers, but before she could come up with an excuse for looking into Barnes, her dad cut her short.

"Sorry, Em. I'm gonna to have to let you go. Got to stop your mom before she burns the house down." The dial tone sounded in her ear.

Emily stared at the receiver, puzzled. What was with her mom and fire lately? Discouraged by her dad's explanation and reminder to butt out, Emily put her laptop away for the day. The pain in her arm was making it hard to concentrate anyway. She gulped down a pain pill along with some cold fried chicken, surfing the channels. Lulled by the drama of daytime talk shows, she dozed off on the couch. In her dreams, she was having a confrontation with Mr. Barnes, but before she could accuse him of murder, someone was calling to her. She turned, distracted, and Barnes slipped away. Emily fought her way to consciousness as someone continued to call her name and gently shake her shoulder. When she finally managed to pry open her eyelids, sticky with sleep, Tad was looking down at her, a frown on his face.

Emily tried to sit up and groaned. Her arm ached, her head felt like it was stuffed with cotton, and she could only imagine the bed head she had going on. She tried to surreptitiously wipe drool from the corner of her mouth before Tad could see it. He continued to frown at her as he switched on the lamp by the couch. "What time is it?" Emily croaked, then cleared her throat.

Tad tucked a pillow behind her head and one under her arm. "Almost six," he answered. "I came straight here from school, but you were sleeping so peacefully, I didn't want to disturb you. But then you started muttering and thrashing around. I thought you might be having a nightmare, so I woke you up. You okay?"

"Yeah, sorry. Must be the painkillers. You didn't have to come back tonight, you know."

Tad kneeled down in front of the couch. "I know I didn't have to. I wanted to." Emily felt a part of her heart begin to ooze like melted butter on hot toast. She tried to tear her gaze from Tad's, but the moment stretched on. She was sure this was it. Tad was finally going to kiss her, but then he abruptly stood up. "Hope you're hungry," he announced with forced cheerfulness, "because supper is in the oven."

Emily bit back her disappointment as she sniffed the air. "Smells amazing. I'm starved." She pushed frantically at her hair as Tad disappeared into the kitchen. He was back in moments with a steaming slice of her favorite Canadian bacon and chicken pizza. When she quirked an eyebrow, he caved. "Okay, I might have picked up a pie on the way home and reheated it."

Emily smiled her gratitude. "Homemade or not, my stomach and I thank you." She dug in, not caring when cheese dripped down her chin. She figured if her looks hadn't run Tad off by now, a little messy eating wouldn't bother him either. She seemed to be right, as he also had strings of cheese drooping between his slice and his mouth.

"Good," he mumbled. After swallowing, he said, "The kids really missed you today. I assured everyone you were fine, but Principal Matthews wanted me to tell you that you could have as many days off as you need."

"That's nice of him, but I'm ready to get back. I miss the kids, too."

Tad nodded his understanding. "I figured as much, but I promised to pass on the word."

"Did Mr. Barnes ask about me?" Emily asked, trying to reign in her sarcasm.

Tad looked nonplussed. "Not directly, no. You still intent on making him a murderer?"

Emily ignored his own dose of sarcasm, instead filling him in on what she had discovered about Barnes while researching today. She ended by saying, "So what if Jim had found out about Barnes's past, and maybe even that his bad conduct had carried over to Ellington, and he was blackmailing him? Then Barnes got tired of paying, or refused to pay, and took Jim out."

"I think it's time for another pain pill and that you should leave this alone. The police are perfectly capable of doing their jobs on their own." Tad carried their plates to the kitchen and then settled down with a stack of papers to grade.

Emily snarled. "You sound like my dad."

"Your dad is a very smart man, so I take that as a compliment." Emily frowned at Tad's smug tone but decided to let the matter drop. Gathering up her own stack of grading, she tried to whittle it down, but after several attempts of crabbing her comments in the margins of the paper she was grading with her left hand, she gave up. Tad was intent on his work, so she shuffled off to bed, figuring she would need the rest for her first day back at school tomorrow. Unfortunately, sleep eluded her. She wasn't sure if it was her worries about Barnes that were keeping her awake, or the fact that she had slept the day away. But combined with her awareness of Tad in the next room, the effect was that she was kept tossing and turning through the darkest hours of the night.

CHAPTER ELEVEN

———

Emily smacked her alarm and pulled the covers over her head, seriously debating calling in again. She could hear Tad banging around in the kitchen and humming something cheerful. She rolled her eyes up to stare at the ceiling, but the smell of frying bacon had her lowering the covers below her nose. She was contemplating the giant step from comfy bed to cold floor when Tad's head popped around the doorframe, looking altogether too handsome and too awake for this early in the morning. Emily yanked the covers firmly back under her chin, swiping at eye crusties. Tad smiled at her and continued into the room, carrying a still-steaming plate. "Thought you might like some breakfast before I left today."

Emily snaked one hand free and snagged a piece of bacon. No one had ever brought her breakfast in bed before, unless you counted her mom when she was little and stayed home sick from school. And then it hit her. "I'm still going to school today, but nice try," she informed Tad. He heaved a sigh and turned to the door.

"It was worth a try," he mumbled, and then louder, "Be ready to leave in twenty then."

The second he was out of the room, Emily threw back the covers and scurried to the bathroom, turning back for one more piece of bacon. Fighting through another miserable shower that consisted of rigorous calisthenics to keep from getting her cast wet left Emily in a worse mood than normal for morning. Her attempts at applying makeup left-handed left her near tears, so she compensated by picking out a cute outfit that would help boost her mood. She was slipping on her last kitten heel when Tad knocked on the doorframe.

"Ready to go?" he asked. Emily admired his teal sweater and black slacks, thinking he looked yummy enough to eat. If they had had math teachers like Tad when she was in school, she might be an accountant today. She realized Tad was watching her stare at him, so she quickly checked for drool. She was good to go. Or so she thought. Tad was frowning and blocking the doorway.

"What?" Emily asked him, confused.

"Your shoes," he told her, pointing at her feet as if she might not understand what he was referring to.

"What's wrong with my shoes?" Emily frowned down at her favorite pair of kitten heels in a houndstooth print. She thought they went perfectly with her steel-gray trousers, black turtleneck, and matching houndstooth scarf.

"You already have one broken arm. And let's be honest, Pit, you're not the most graceful person in the world. Don't you think you should ditch the heels? At least until your arm heals?"

Emily sniffed. Clearly, Tad underestimated her love affair with shoes. "That is the most ridiculous thing I've ever heard. Mom swears I took my first steps in heels." She brushed past him, trying not to notice the rich, woodsy smell of his cologne. Instead, she scooped up her bag and waited by the door, tapping one of her lethal heels. Tad rolled his eyes but didn't say anything more on the matter, which Emily felt was very wise of him.

Stepping outside, she came up short when she realized her beloved PT wasn't in the driveway. She swallowed hard. "I guess I need to go car shopping," she said in a small voice. Tad rubbed her arm sympathetically. "But that can wait. Let's roll." She might have sniffled another time or two, but then she set her mind on the day ahead. Today was the day that she was determined to get the goods on Barnes once and for all.

* * *

Emily let herself into her classroom, slightly breathless from all the hugs and well wishes she had received on her way up the stairs. It was good to be back. Setting her bag on her desk chair, she pulled out her lesson plan book. Glancing inside, she groaned. There was no way she could avoid the copy room any longer. The copies of the quiz she had planned had to be made today. She was trying to work up the nerve to make the short trek, when a soft knock at her door had her jumping. She let out a high-pitched squeal that sounded more like she was choking, and then was annoyed at her own nervousness. Looking up, she saw a fringe of dark hair outside the door. She waved Stevie in. He toed the floor, hesitant to speak. Emily waited him out, knowing he would say what he had come to say when he was good and ready.

Finally, he flipped his hair out of his eyes and looked straight into hers. "I'm glad you're okay," he said softly.

Emily blinked rapidly to keep the tears from showing, but she knew her voice was gruff when she answered, "I am too. Who else would teach you guys about mythology?" She had tried to play it lightly but was surprised when Stevie vehemently shook his head.

"No, I don't mean I'm glad you're okay because you're one of our teachers. I'm glad because there has been enough violence. I'm glad because you're a nice person. I'm glad because you believe that Ms. Burning is innocent."

This was the most Stevie had ever spoken to her at one time, so Emily was unsure of which of his comments to respond to first. She settled on, "Why do you believe Ms. Burning is innocent?"

"She was going to try and talk my mom out of making me quit football. She felt it was good for me to be involved in the school. She...she understood me." Stevie looked so forlorn that Emily wanted to hug him.

"Why did your mom want you to quit the team?" Emily was curious if his reply would be the same as his mom's.

"She felt I was spending too much time on football and not enough time on schoolwork. She was pretty upset that my grades were so low. She thought Coach kept us focused only on the game." He paused to look at her intently. "But you know that Coach took our academics seriously. He had been on my case about my grades."

His comment that Helen was going to try to keep Stevie on the football team now caused her some worry. In her experience, Helen always championed the child. But even if she felt Stevie should remain on the team, had she argued with Coach about the grades Stevie was carrying? Would they have met late at night at the school to discuss the matter? Barnes said he overheard them arguing earlier. But he also said they mentioned the police. The police would have no place in a conversation about grades. The police had to mean something more serious, possibly something more violent, and the way Coach had died could definitely be labeled violent. Emily gave a mental head shake. No. Helen would never resort to violence. She became aware that Stevie was watching her closely, as if trying to read her mind. Time to focus on the main issue here: Stevie's grades.

"Why do you feel your grades are slipping, Stevie? When I spoke with your mom, she mentioned that you were normally strong in academics, especially English."

"You talked to my mom?" Stevie's eyes were big. But before she could answer, he shrugged and said, "I'm sick of moving."

"Have you moved a lot?" Emily knew the real estate market was fickle at best. Arlene had indicated that they had been moving so that she could get better jobs. Emily couldn't imagine the burden of raising a child alone. And it was clear that Arlene wanted only the best for Stevie.

"Yeah. Mom's job demands it, I guess. At least that's what she always tells me. She promised that our last move would be the final one. I liked it in Iowa. But now here we are in Ellington. She promised me this would be the final move, too. I know she wants the best for me, but I'm really sick and tired of making new friends and learning new ropes." Stevie went back to scuffing the toe of his black Converse on the tile floor. "I don't mean to sound ungrateful. I have the best mom in the world. Really. And I promised her I would do better in school." He once again met her eyes. "I'll do better. Promise."

Emily nodded. She believed him. She knew she was short on time to get her copies made before the final bell, but Stevie's comment about Iowa echoed in her mind. Jim had also come to Ellington from Iowa. Coincidence? She tried to sound casual as she asked, "Where in Iowa did you move from?

Peculiar Bluffs? I know some people there." Well, she knew the principal and Elsie. That qualified as "some," right?

"Nah. We lived in a small town outside of Cedar Rapids for my junior high years. Look, I better be going. I'll see you in class." With a quick smile, he slipped back out the door, shutting it quietly behind him. Guess it really was coincidence. Foiled again. Turning back to her desk, Emily squared her shoulders and sucked in an audible breath of courage. The copy room awaited. She was about to make the world's fastest copies.

* * *

Once she had faced her fears, the rest of the morning felt like smooth sailing. The students seemed glad to have her back, and it was comforting to be in a familiar routine. Her students laughed at her clumsy attempts to write on the board left-handed, but the mythology unit seemed to be a big success. Stevie paid close attention during lecture, and when they began their review for the quiz, he was the first one to raise his hand. Emily felt buoyed by her success, and despite her heavy cast, she practically bounced into the teachers' lounge at lunchtime. As she shoved a piece of leftover pizza in the microwave to reheat, she was thrilled to see that only she and Barnes had made it in for lunch so far. She flopped down on the chair opposite his and gave him a blinding smile. "Sure is nice to be back," she said in her most annoyingly chipper voice.

Barnes barely glanced up from his three-bean salad. No wonder the man was so small—he ate like a bird. "Yes, glad to see you are up and about." Emily had never heard a more insincere comment in her life. She bared her teeth. She was determined to break down Barnes.

"Of course, it's a little hard to get around without my wheels. My PT was one of the great loves of my life." She heaved a dramatic sigh. "I'm sure you understand," she continued.

Barnes blinked at her, reinforcing his reptilian image. Emily waited for his tongue to dart out and snag an errant fly. "Why would I understand?" he slowly asked.

"Why? Well, we've all seen that awesome new car of yours. Had to set you back a chunk, huh?"

Emily had never known a man who didn't love to talk about his new toys, but Barnes just shrugged and went back to his beans. Emily chewed furiously, trying to come up with a comment that would goad him into responding. A couple more teachers had drifted in, and under the low murmur of conversation around them, she asked quietly, "What was it you drove before? A dark SUV, wasn't it?" Actually, Emily couldn't remember what Barnes had driven before. This was a Hail Mary pass. She watched Barnes from under her eyelashes. His eyes flicked up to meet hers, and he gave her a sickly smile.

"Like the one that ran you off the road?" Emily gulped. She hadn't been as subtle as she had thought. "No, Ms. Taylor, I drove a white S-10 pickup." And with that, he dumped the remains of his salad in the trash and swept out the door. Emily glared after him, chomping on her pizza.

* * *

The rest of the afternoon went quickly, but Emily was more focused on her conversation with Barnes than on mythology. She was gratified that the students were enjoying the new unit, but she was irritated at her strikeout with that slimy toad, Barnes. The fact that he knew what kind of vehicle had run her off the road was disconcerting. Of course, that information was sure to have been in the news, but the fact that he threw it in her face seemed intentional. Did he mean it as a threat? More than ever, Emily was convinced that Barnes had something to do with Jim's death.

By the time the bell rang, signaling the end of the school day, Emily was exhausted. Her arm throbbed, and she was ready to head home to her pain pills and soft bed. She hadn't seen Tad since that morning, but now she needed to find him for a ride. She was locking her classroom door when Principal Matthews stopped by to check on her. She reassured him that she was fine and ready to be back at school. Even that short interlude added to the pain in her arm. She pushed through the door into the teachers' lounge and was relieved to see Tad there, nursing a cold soda. Without a word, he popped a top for her, and she collapsed onto the couch. Swinging a chair around to straddle, Tad studied her as he drank deep on his soda. "You look pale," he said with a frown.

"I'm okay," she responded between gulps, "just tired. It was a good day. Really," she reiterated at his raised eyebrows. "But my arm is a little sore. I'm ready for my pain pills, so I was hoping you were ready to head out."

"Let me gather my stuff." Tad stood and swung the chair back around. As he shoved it under the table, he said, with his back still to her, "I heard you were having a serious conversation with Barnes at lunch. There might even have been reports that you ran him out of the room."

Emily tossed her head defiantly. "Since when did you succumb to listening to the gossip mill?" she asked Tad's back.

"Since you almost got yourself killed," he said loudly, spinning to face her. Emily was taken aback at the fierceness in his look. She grabbed one of the couch pillows and hugged it to her in an unconscious gesture of comfort. Tad pushed a lock of hair off of his forehead and sank down on the tabletop. "I'm worried about you, Pit," he said more softly. Emily nodded. She wasn't sure what to say. The silence between them stretched, and she eventually glanced askance at Tad to gauge his temperament. He was staring so intently at her that the saliva in her mouth dried up, sticking her tongue to the roof of her mouth as effectively as a peanut butter sandwich.

When Tad only continued to stare, she hugged the pillow tighter and asked, "What?" Her voice sounded harsh and strident in the silence, but Tad said nothing. In one smooth move, he lunged forward and ripped the pillow out of her arms. Emily let out an exclamation of surprise and half stood, instinctively reaching to grab the pillow back. Tad held it out of her reach, examining it closely under the fluorescent lights. Emily settled back on the couch, miffed at his childish behavior. At her sniff, Tad whirled toward her and shoved the pillow under her nose.

She reared back. "What is your deal?" she asked, irritated to the extreme.

"Look!" he said. Emily looked around. She didn't see anything out of the norm. They were the only two people in the lounge, and everything seemed to be in place.

Tad shook his head and wiggled the pillow. "No. Look," he said more forcefully.

Emily examined the pillow closely. The brown-and-orange floral motif was as repugnant as ever, but beyond that, she had no idea what she was looking for. She looked at Tad in exasperation. "Yep. Ugly as ever. So what gives?"

Tad tapped a finger to a particularly putrid brown flower. "What do you see?"

"World's ugliest couch pillow?"

Tad huffed out a breath that stirred the hair on his forehead. "No," he said patiently.

Emily's confusion must have shown in her eyes. Tad eased down beside her and pointed at the same ugly flower. "Em, look closer. What do you see?"

Emily began to seriously wonder if Tad had cracked from lack of sleep and worry over her, but she looked. And this time, she saw what Tad was pointing at. "Is that…is that…" Her brain recoiled, and her mouth refused to form the words.

"Yes." Tad gave a definite nod. "*That* is blood." Emily felt all of her own blood rush to her head as Tad pushed her head between her knees. "Breathe," he commanded her. "We don't have time for you to pass out right now. I need to get this to Detective Welks."

Emily raised her head enough to watch Tad grab a trash bag out of the cabinet over the sink and bag the pillow. Feeling a bit steadier, she pushed to her feet. "If you're going to see Detective Gangly-Arms, so am I." When Tad started to shake his head, Emily added, "After all, you're my ride."

Tad rolled his eyes but grabbed her bag and the pillow. "Come on, then. Let me grab my keys and we'll head out. Don't say anything. We don't want to tip anyone off unnecessarily." He didn't name names, but as Tad gathered his keys and locked his classroom door, Emily found herself staring down the hallway at Barnes's classroom. Was she staring at the door of a room that housed a murderer?

CHAPTER TWELVE

———

Detective Gangly-Arms led Emily and Tad back to a desk in the far corner of a busy, cluttered room. He studiously took notes while Tad pointed out the blood stain on the couch pillow and explained how they had accidentally discovered it. Emily bounced on the edge of her seat, gnawing at a ragged fingernail. Could this discovery be significant in proving Helen's innocence? She was afraid to ask, to burst this bubble of hope that was welling inside her. As if sensing her unasked question, Gangly-Arms addressed his next comment to her. "Ms. Taylor"—his expression was grave—"did you see this pillow or any other out-of-place object near Mr. Layton's body at the time of discovery?"

Emily strained to recall details of the scene, but her memories were clouded by the stark terror that filled her at the sight of Jim's lifeless body. "No, not that I can remember. I'm sorry," she added.

Gangly-Arms nodded in understanding. "It's okay. It was a long shot anyway. Whoever murdered Mr. Layton was very careful to cover his or her tracks."

"So have you found the murder weapon?" Tad asked, scooting forward in his own chair.

"If you mean, have we found the item used to strike a blow to the back of Mr. Layton's head, then the answer is no. If you mean, have we found the item used to murder him, then it would appear you have been the one to do that."

Emily turned wide eyes on Tad and could see by the expression on his face that he was as clueless as she. "Excuse me?" Tad asked the detective.

For the first time, Emily could see the weariness and frustration etched in the young detective's face, but the firmness of his jaw and the clenched fists at the end of his incredibly long arms showed his determination to figure out exactly what had happened to Jim. He looked them each in the eye, weighing his words with care. "The coroner's report on Mr. Layton came through earlier this afternoon. It turns out that while Mr. Layton obviously sustained a debilitating blow to the back of his head, the actual cause of his death was asphyxiation." Emily's heart dropped and her hand unconsciously flew to her throat, her own breaths feeling tight and shallow in her grief-filled chest. Hitting someone over the head in a fit of anger and causing his death was horrible, but somehow, the thought of holding something over someone's face until he took his final breath seemed even more hideous, more personal, more…everything. The thought that she had been hugging to her chest the very pillow that might have smothered Jim's last breath caused revulsion to well up within her, choking her. She was dimly aware of Tad rubbing comforting circles on her upper back, and she concentrated her whole being on that feeling, that tangible touch of understanding. Slowly, her breathing became more normal, and she was once again able to tune in to the conversation. She sent Tad a grateful smile, and he gave her a small nod in return. Gangly-Arms was explaining, somewhat shamefacedly, that they had not yet determined the item used to asphyxiate Jim. The thought had initially been that the killer took the item with him or her to dispose of it elsewhere. But now, with the discovery of the pillow, it seemed the murder weapon had been hiding in plain sight the whole time. He assured them both that the blood on the pillow would be tested for a match to Jim's as soon as possible.

Emily's mind played a black-and-white film wherein Barnes smothered a stricken Jim with the ugly couch pillow. Emily truly believed that Barnes was the culprit, but the highlight reel in her mind pointed out a salient fact that could halt the rolling film. Jim was a large, strong man. Barnes was a scrawny, slimy toad. There would be no way that Barnes could overpower Jim and smother him with a pillow. Jim could have swatted Barnes away like the flies he likely dined upon. She clenched the edge of the detective's desk as she eagerly asked, "How much strength would it require for someone to asphyxiate a man of Jim's size?" Her knuckles turned white as she waited for the detective to consider her question.

"In all actuality, it probably wouldn't have required much strength at all to smother Mr. Layton. The blow to the back of the head likely rendered him unconscious. The murderer would only need enough strength to strike the back of his head and then roll him over." Gangly-Arms sounded regretful, but Emily was elated at the thought that she was one step closer to proving Barnes's guilt and exonerating Helen.

She was about to expound on her theory about the smarmy Barnes, when Tad interrupted. "What about the lack of history for Jim Layton? I did some looking online, but before he showed up in Peculiar Bluffs, Iowa, the man's life was a closed book. How does a person in this day and age manage to exist for so long without leaving some kind of electronic footprint?"

"Interesting that you should ask," Gangly-Arms answered, leaning back in his desk chair and crossing his arms behind his head. "After running his prints, we determined that Mr. Layton's actual name was Jim Olsen. Does that ring any bells for you?" When both Tad and Emily shook their heads, he continued. "I can't imagine why he changed his name. The guy had no criminal record. We've traced him back to a school in Ithaca, New York, where he taught before moving to Iowa. We know that he had a brother, but the principal at the school that we spoke to was new to the district and couldn't provide us with any further information. This lead developed just this morning, so we are still in the process of ferreting out information. If you hear or remember anything about a Jim Olsen, please be sure and contact me. I hope to locate the brother by the end of the day." Gangly-Arms stared at his relatively clutter-free desktop, and Emily figured he was not looking forward to breaking such sad news to Jim's brother. Assuring him that they would contact him with any further information, Emily and Tad left the hustle and bustle of the station and stepped back out into the weak October sunlight. Emily wrapped her arm around her middle, aching all over again for Jim's senseless death and Helen's disappearance. Where could Helen *be*?

Tad slipped an arm around her shoulders and hugged her to his side. "Penny for your thoughts?" he asked lightly, tucking an errant strand of her chestnut bob behind her ear.

"I was wondering where Helen could possibly be," she answered, not meeting his eyes.

"And?" Tad prompted.

"And..." she drew the word out. "I was also contemplating how to best prove that Barnes is the one behind all of this."

Tad released her shoulders, along with a pent-up breath of frustration. "Pit, I think you have blinders on. However, since you seem hell bent on proving his guilt, I wish you would stay with your parents until this is all over. I would stay tonight, but I have a Mathletes' practice this evening that will probably run long, as we're gearing up for a competition. I'd hate to wake you by getting back late. Want me to call your parents?"

Emily shook her head. She was ready for some peace and quiet. "I'll be fine, Tad. I'm perfectly capable of taking care of myself." She made sure her voice sounded more convinced then she felt. Time away from Tad would allow her to think more clearly. Tad looked skeptical, but he nodded.

Back in the car, he said, "You know, I'm only a phone call away." It was not a question.

Emily gave him a small smile. "I *do* know. You have definitely proven what a great friend you are these past couple of days to put up with me. Thank you for everything."

"Well, that's what friends are for," Tad replied, never taking his eyes off the road. Was it Emily's imagination, or did Tad sound a little sardonic? She watched him carefully, but his profile revealed nothing. Before she could decide whether or not to say anything further, they were pulling into her drive.

Tad gathered his things and loaded them into his car. He made sure Emily was comfortably settled on the couch with a cold drink, her phone, and the remote control. He seemed to be stalling his departure, and Emily felt like she was treading on shaky ground. Tad was watching her closely, but her tongue was tangled in a knot. The silence swelled around them. Tad finally leaned over and planted a soft kiss on her forehead. Before she could react, he was out the door. Emily tried to ignore the pang in her chest as she watched him drive away. She had gotten used to having him here, and suddenly the apartment seemed too quiet and too large without his presence. Determined to shake her morose mood, she stabbed a button, bringing the TV flickering to life. Then she called her mom.

After reassuring her mom several times that she was truly feeling fine, her mom expressed extreme displeasure that Tad would no longer be staying with her. She wasn't sure if her mom was more worried about her well-being or in making some kind of match between her and Tad. Either way, she changed the subject and described their trip to the police station with the blood-stained pillow. Her mom punctuated her recital of the day's events with exclamations of shock and dismay. When Emily mentioned that Jim's real name had actually been Jim Olsen, her mom stopped her.

"Jim Olsen? That sounds familiar."

"Really?" Emily scooted up on the couch cushions, clutching the phone tighter.

"I can't recall off the top of my head. I'll give you a ring if something pops later, okay?" And at that, her mom was gone, presumably to ruminate on where she had heard that name before. Knowing her mom, she would probably call her in the middle of the night, or from the shower, when the elusive reference came flooding back. In the meantime, Emily next called to check on Gabby. Emily was thrilled that Gabby was up and about and able to talk to her herself.

"Gabby, I'm so very, very sorry. I can't ever apologize enough. I never should have gotten you involved. I'm sure Greg would like to kill me, but he's been very kind. Are you sure you're okay?" She would have continued, but Gabby cut off her flow of apologies with a soft laugh.

"Em, you didn't put me anywhere I didn't want to be. There's no way you could have known that a psychopath would try to run us off the road. Any news on that, by the way?"

"No," Emily reported, sipping at her soda. "But Tad and I did discover something interesting today." She filled Gabby in on the blood-stained pillow and the alternate name. Then she returned to her favorite topic: Barnes the Villain.

"So," she concluded, "I want to do some recon on Barnes. I was thinking a stakeout…" She trailed off, but Gabby pounced on her words.

"And you need a car," Gabby reasoned. "While I need out of this house before I go insane. I love Greg, but he's smothering me with all his care. I'll be there as soon as it's dark."

"Are you sure? Greg would be furious if he knew what we had planned."

"What Greg doesn't know can't hurt him, right? See you later." Gabby clicked off and Emily was reminded once again why they were best friends—a shared love of mysteries, ice cream, and impulsive, spontaneous acts.

* * *

A couple of hours later found Emily and Gabby parked down the block on the opposite side of the street from Barnes's little, white, ranch-style house. The outside was austere, definitely lacking in character. If Emily could have picked out the perfect house for the slimeball, this would be it. She slurped noisily at the fresh soda Gabby had come packing. As the darkness crept closer, Emily filled Gabby in on all the latest details, avoiding too much mention of Tad. She could feel Gabby's burning curiosity scorching the air around them, but she delved into a detailed evaluation of the latest *Bachelor* episodes to stave off any questions. Gabby knew her well enough not to push for details about her time with Tad, and Emily was grateful. Something was definitely developing or changing or something, but she wasn't yet ready to examine it too closely. Once she tore every moment, every look, every word between her and Tad apart and came to a decision about what she wanted, it would be time to act. And what if she was wrong? What if Tad still saw her as nothing more than a friend, the daughter of his mentor, and an occasional thorn in his side? Having drained her soda, she flipped off the plastic lid and crunched a piece of ice. The munching sound was deafening in the small space. Gabby started and gave a nervous laugh. She was scouring the floor behind her seat.

"What are you looking for?" Emily asked, thinking that with the detritus floating around Gabby's minivan, she could plausibly be mining for gold.

"The girls have a play set of binoculars around here somewhere that actually work, but all I'm coming up with is stale Cheerios."

"Binoculars. Good idea. Wish I'd thought of it." Emily made a mental note to pick a pair up from her dad. He was a keen bird watcher and kept several sets in his shop.

Gabby twisted her body back around, giving up the search. Instead she rummaged through her purse, coming up with a couple of granola bars. After devouring those, Gabby unearthed a bottle of teal-blue nail polish and gave Emily a quick manicure by flashlight, also found in Gabby's treasure chest of a purse, while they waited. Waving the nails on her uninjured arm in the air and pointlessly attempting to blow on the nails of her casted arm to help dry them, Emily checked the clock. "Okay," she finally admitted. "I have no idea what we're waiting for, and I'm starving. Maybe we should call it a night?"

Gabby's response was to yank Emily's arm hard enough to have her falling over the console, banging her head on the dash as she did so. "What the…" she spluttered.

Gabby hushed her, motioning out the window on her side of the minivan. A dark SUV was creeping down the street, and as they watched, it pulled into Barnes's driveway. Emily forgot about the pain in her head as her heart tattooed a painful rhythm in her chest and up into her throat. "Gabby," she croaked. "A dark SUV."

"I know," Gabby said grimly, never taking her eyes off the vehicle. They both held their breath as they watched a shadowy figure slip out of the driver's side. From their vantage point, the person seemed on the small side, but gender could not be determined as the figure had a large hood pulled over his or her head. The figure opened the back driver's side door and removed a large briefcase, then proceeded toward the house. As the figure neared the door, he or she slipped a hand into a pocket. Instinct took over and Emily slid into the floorboard, covering her head with her uninjured arm. "What are you doing?" Gabby hissed.

"Gun!" Emily yelped.

To her surprise, Gabby chuckled. "Unless the gun has a flashlight attached to it, I think we're safe. It looks like a cell phone." Emily slithered back up into her seat, glad the darkness hid her furious blush. But really, who could blame her for being cautious after all they had been through in the past week?

The figure seemed to be talking into said cell phone but tucked it back into a pocket as Barnes opened the door. Emily ducked again, this time out of an irrational fear that Barnes would be able to see them through the darkness. And he did indeed glance furtively around before motioning the figure inside. As the door closed on the two figures, Gabby rounded on her. "Now what?" she demanded.

Emily hated to point out the elephant in the car, so to speak, but the question begged to be asked. "Could that have been Helen?"

Gabby hesitated. "Whoever it was is definitely small enough to be her. And that *is* a dark SUV. But without taking a closer look, who can be sure?"

"You said it," Emily agreed, already reaching for the door handle.

"Wait!" Gabby screeched. Once again, she fumbled through her cavernous purse, this time producing a dark scarf that she deftly tied over Emily's blindingly white cast.

"Smart thinking," Emily nodded approvingly. "Is there anything you don't have in that purse of yours?"

"Doubt it," Gabby assured her. "Let's roll out." Emily hid a smile at the grave note in Gabby's tone.

"Yes, commander." Emily gave her a smart salute and eased out of her side of the minivan. She considered rolling over the hood of the minivan in an imitation of Channing Tatum in the remake of *21 Jump Street*, but then she realized Gabby was already across the street, crouching next to the SUV, motioning her forward. She made a furtive dash to join Gabby, reminding herself not to enjoy this all quite so much. This was a serious mission. Whoever drove this SUV could be the same person who ran them off the road. This sobering thought had her crouching even further down. She and Gabby made their way around the Tahoe, closely examining the front and back bumpers. It was the same color as Helen's, but there was no discernable damage, which Emily adroitly pointed out.

Gabby countered, "The damage could already have been fixed." Emily nodded, but she was skeptical. Granted, she didn't know much about cars, but this one looked brand new. There were no personal items in the car, the interior spotless.

Emily motioned to the windshield. "Helen always has a Scentsy hanger on her rearview mirror."

Gabby nodded. Again she asked, "Now what?"

Emily frowned. "I can't believe that Helen would be in cahoots with someone like Barnes, but we need to see what else we can find out."

Gabby gave her a sympathetic smile. "I know you don't want Helen to be guilty, and"—she held up her hand when Emily started to interrupt—"and I don't think she's guilty either, but we need to be objective. This might be Helen's vehicle still, and what if she's actually here to harm Barnes? He could have been blackmailing Helen *and* Jim. If you're right, and Barnes killed Jim, Helen could have left town to avoid facing the same fate. Maybe she's here to convince Barnes to turn himself in, or..." She left the rest unsaid, but Emily could follow the direction of her thoughts. Or, Helen could be here to eliminate the problem.

"What could Barnes possibly have on Helen that would be worth blackmailing her over?" she asked Gabby.

Gabby shrugged. "I have no idea. How well do we ever really know the inner workings of someone else's life? If Helen did kill Layton, Barnes could have been a witness. You said yourself that Barnes practically lives at the school. But, honestly? I have no idea. Maybe..." Gabby cut off in midsentence. "Did you hear that?"

Emily strained to listen, but all she heard was the sigh of the wind through the trees. And the low moan of a...what? "Yep. What is that?" Whatever it was, it had the hair on the back of Emily's neck standing at attention. There was no reply. Emily glanced behind her and frantically whispered, "Gabby!" as she was nowhere in sight.

"Over here," came a hiss from the shadows next to the house. Emily crab-walked over to the sound and watched as Gabby strained on her tiptoes, trying to see in a side window.

"All the windows have shades on them. You'd think the guy was paranoid someone would try to see in." Gabby looked so irritated in the dim light provided by a low-hanging moon that Emily forbore to mention the obvious. Given their current occupation, Barnes had every right to be paranoid. Emily crept along behind Gabby, peeking in at each window they came to. The low moaning sound continued, and half of Emily hoped Barnes was suffering a fate worse than death, as befitted the toad, but the other, more sensible half, hoped to find nothing as they continued their search.

The sound was definitely getting louder as they rounded the far side of the house. Gabby bounced around like a spastic cheerleader, trying to find a window she could peer into. At the last window on the far side of the house, they finally found a crack in the blinds. Gabby motioned for Emily to boost her up so she could get a better view. Emily shook her head and motioned to her cast. Gabby pantomimed frustration, stomping her foot on the ground. Looking around, she spotted a small flowerpot discarded in the well of a darkened basement window. Gabby perched precariously on the pot with one foot, grasping the sill with both hands. She turned to Emily and said in a stage whisper, "It's an office." Then they were both silent, listening intently for any further sound. The moaning and groaning resumed, louder now. Emily slipped her phone out of her pocket, gripping it tightly in her left hand, ready to dial 9-1-1. Although she truly despised Barnes, she was now terrified that he actually was dying a painful death while they lurked outside like Peeping Toms, doing nothing to help.

Gabby hopped off the flowerpot so she could better whisper to Emily. She reached out a hand to push Emily's cell phone away. Emily gaped at her. "What are you doing? We need to call for help. He could be dying in there!"

To Emily's astonishment, Gabby shook her head. "Or?" She left the word hanging, raising both eyebrows and waggling them suggestively.

Emily was not following. "Or?"

"Or," Gabby repeated, "he's in there having sex."

For a full minute, Emily gaped like a fish out of water. The image Gabby had planted in her brain seared her retinas.

Blinking away the white spots, she swallowed down the bile that had risen in her throat. Gabby giggled at her expression but then turned serious. "We have to find out for sure. One way or the other."

Emily grimaced. "Do we have to? Can't we just call the cops and run?"

Gabby stared at her but said nothing. The censure in her gaze was not lost on Emily. "Okay, okay. I dragged you into this, so I'll risk being scarred for life. I need something sturdier and taller to stand on than that puny flowerpot, though." They once again scanned the side yard for something to give them a leg up, but seeing nothing, Gabby dashed off to her minivan. Emily hoped against hope that she was not finally giving up on all these shenanigans and leaving her to fend for herself. She needn't have worried, though, as Gabby was soon back at her side, toting a child's potty seat.

"How fitting," Emily said drily. "Do I even want to ask why this was in your van?" Emily gave the object a wide berth, wondering how much use it had seen.

Gabby huffed out an indignant breath. "You have no idea how trying potty training is," she whispered furiously. "Especially with girls. It's not like they can go on the side of the road like boys can. This is our solution. But don't worry—neither of the twins has taken the slightest interest in this yet. Pull-Ups are still their preferred means."

Emily placed the potty-chair under the window and put her phone back in her pocket to free her hand. She was as prepared as she could be to risk her mental well-being. "After this, I may wish I had on Pull-Ups myself," she whispered down to Gabby, and then she was peering inside.

At first, all she could see was a wall of books and a small fireplace. She was surprised to find herself filled with envy at a room in Barnes's house. This was the perfect, cozy library. She strained to see further to her left. A table came into view, and Emily leaned closer to the window, flattening her nose against it. She could now see three-quarters of the table and recognized it for what it was—a massage table. A small Asian woman kneaded the pale flesh of Barnes's back as he lay stomach-down and, thankfully, covered by a sheet. In a flash of understanding, Emily realized that the figure entering Barnes's house had not been carrying a briefcase after all, but a portable massage table instead. Portable appeared to be the word of the day.

Emily snickered and turned, giddy with relief and ready to make their getaway. They might not have found out any dirt on Barnes, but at least this night had provided them with some good laughs. Gabby was yanking at her sweater, anxious to know what Emily had seen. Emily had the first words on her lips when the phone in her pocket picked that particular moment to blare out her signature "Crazy Train" ringtone. Emily froze, and everything seemed to move in slow motion. She fumbled her phone out and tried to stab the reject button before dropping to the ground. She torqued her body to look back at the massage table. Despite her hope that the sound had not been heard inside, Barnes had jumped to his feet. The sheet that had been covering him slid to the floor like a shedding skin. In one horrific flash, Barnes stood in front of the window, in all his birthday-suit glory. Emily stumbled backward in horror, and without waiting on Gabby, sprinted toward the minivan, hoping to outrun a sight that would scar her for life. Without looking back, she could hear Gabby's footfalls pounding behind her, the potty-chair banging against her leg but not slowing her down.

They propelled themselves into the van, and Gabby cranked the key. In seconds, they were flying down the road, giggling madly, like two teenagers sneaking out of the house. Emily knew pure adrenaline had them laughing at their panic, but she couldn't stop the chuckles. As she choked out the story of Barnes leaping from the massage table, Gabby dissolved in waves of laughter, and soon, they were both wiping at dripping eyes. In mid-laugh, Gabby turned huge eyes on Emily. "What?" Emily asked, startled into seriousness by Gabby's expression.

"Your ringtone," Gabby breathed.

Emily waved a dismissive hand. "I know," she commiserated. "I can't believe I didn't put my phone on silent. Rookie mistake."

"No, that's not what I mean. Barnes heard your phone ringing."

"Right..." Emily drawled, wondering where this was headed.

"You work with Barnes." Gabby's eyes were now filled with worry.

"Right again?" Emily began to feel a niggling of worry, but she still had no idea what Gabby was concerned about.

"That's been your ringtone forever, and—"

"I know. I'll change it. I happen to really like that song, though." Emily defended her ringtone.

Again Gabby shook her head, dark ringlets escaping from her ponytail and lashing her cheeks. "You've taught with Barnes for several years now. You've had that ringtone for a coon's age. He has to have heard your phone ring before. Even if he didn't see you out the window, he's going to know it was you outside."

"Oh. *Oh*." Emily tapped her fingers on her thigh, the situation no longer hysterically funny. "Maybe he hasn't paid that close attention to my phone. Or maybe he'll think it was a student."

"Sure," Gabby agreed, but Emily detected a note of sarcasm. "All the kids these days are playing 'Crazy Train.'"

Emily swatted her arm. "If you want to throw stones for ridiculousness, how about you sprinting across the yard with a potty-chair? If Barnes looked out the window, I'm pretty sure he won't think a student was lurking around his house with a child's toilet in tow."

"Touché," Gabby responded. "Either way, the damage is done. What do we do to repair it?"

Emily considered a moment, and then she and Gabby came to the same conclusion. "Ice cream."

* * *

Over caramel sundaes at their favorite late-night drive-thru, they debated their next move. "Who was calling you, by the way?" Gabby asked through a mouth of soft-serve vanilla.

Emily dug the offending phone out of her pocket and scrolled through her list of missed calls. "Mom," she answered, hitting the button to return the call.

Her mom answered before the first ring ended, and Emily felt guilty for not checking her phone and calling her back earlier. "Where were you?" Her mom's voice was accusing.

"I'm with Gabby. Grabbing some ice cream and having some girl time. Must not have heard my phone in my purse." Emily winced at the white lie. She hated lying to her parents. Gabby knew it, too, and waved her red spoon at her in a reprimanding manner. Emily ignored her to focus on her mom's words. She was saying something about remembering a news story.

"You remembered what?" she asked her mom.

"Jim Olsen." It took Emily a minute to place the name, as her mind was still wrapped up in her adventures at the toad's house. "I remember where I heard his name."

Emily straightened in her seat. "Where?" she asked anxiously.

"He was in the news, oh, quite a few years ago now. You were probably nine or ten at the time, but I remember I still watched you like a hawk for a long while. A young baby was kidnapped in New York. The search was intense, but the poor mother couldn't handle the strain. She blamed herself and was suffering from postpartum depression. Several months after the kidnapping, she committed suicide. My heart broke for that poor young mother." Her mom's voice was soft.

"So, Jim was the baby's father?" Emily clarified.

"No. Sorry. I think the dad's name was Stephen. Jim was his younger brother. He was the spokesman for the family through much of the investigation. After the mother's suicide, the story slowly faded into obscurity, as they so often do. It's tragic, really."

"What happened to the baby? Was the kidnapper ever found?"

"I don't believe so. I don't remember hearing anything about the baby being returned to his family."

"The baby was a boy?" Emily brushed away Gabby, who was practically sitting in her lap, trying to hear what her mom was saying. She placed the phone on speaker so Gabby could hear too.

"Yes, I believe so. Why, that baby would probably be sixteen or seventeen by now." She didn't add what they were all thinking. That would be the baby's age *if* he had survived.

"If Jim was the brother of a man in New York who lost both his child and his wife, how did he ever end up in Ellington, Missouri?" she asked.

"Good question," her mom answered. "Your dad and I were just discussing that. Unfortunately, now that poor Jim has been murdered, we may never know."

Emily thanked her mom for the information and hung up. The only sound in the minivan was the scraping of their spoons against their plastic ice cream dishes. Emily broke the silence by asking the obvious question. "How does this tie Jim to Helen? Helen didn't have any children. Jim didn't have any children. I would never have guessed Jim had such a sad past. He seemed like such a happy guy. But the principal at Peculiar Bluffs did mention some tragedy in his brother's life."

"But why did he change his last name?" Gabby countered.

"I have no idea. And frankly, I'm too tired to figure it out tonight. Greg will be wondering where you are. Let's call it a night."

Gabby headed the car toward Emily's duplex, but she was hesitant to leave Emily there alone. She was trying to talk her into staying with them for a few days, but Emily wanted the comfort of her own bed. Her life had been in enough upheaval the past week. Emily patted Gabby's arm reassuringly. "I'll be fine. Barnes, if he does know it was me outside, is probably as mortified as I am. I can't see how he fits into this whole mess now, either. He doesn't have any children, and somehow, the fact that Jim changed his name and moved so far from New York after such devastating events in his brother's life has to figure into the equation. I feel like we're back to square one."

"Maybe not," Gabby said in a strangled voice. She had angled the minivan in Emily's drive so that her headlights would shine on the front door. The glare of the lights revealed the picture window in Emily's living room. Emily had closed the blinds and drawn the curtains tight before she had left, but now they were flapping in the breeze. At first, she wondered if she had somehow overlooked an open window. But with all the rain they had been experiencing lately, she didn't think she had had her windows open at all. Gabby flipped her beams up on high and Emily saw what had Gabby so frightened. Her window hadn't been left open—it had been shattered.

CHAPTER THIRTEEN

———

Emily's mind swirled as quickly as the leaves blowing through her newly renovated front window. Without stopping to consider any possible danger, she threw the passenger side door of the minivan open and pounded up the front steps. She paused to fumble for her keys and was lifted bodily off her feet. Gabby's wiry arms held her firm as Emily struggled to free herself.

"Oh, no, you don't," Gabby snapped, towing her back to the minivan with an iron grip on her upper arm.

Emily dug her boots in but found no purchase on the leaf-strewn sidewalk. She spit out a hank of hair that had blown into her mouth and spluttered at Gabby. "Leaves are getting inside. I need to call someone to board this up."

Gabby whipped her around. "What you need to do is call the police."

Emily gaped at Gabby. "Why? They don't board up broken windows," she said stupidly.

"How do you think that window got broken?" Gabby countered.

Emily surveyed her darkened front window and billowing curtains. Gabby was right. She assumed a branch had smashed the window, but it had been a calm night. The wind was just now picking up, and there was no tree branch in sight. Realization dawned.

"Someone broke my window!" she yelled at Gabby, backpedaling to the minivan. Gabby hopped into her side, slamming her hand down on the door locks. Emily's whole body shook violently, and after several failed attempts to dial the police, she mutely handed the phone to Gabby. She listened with half an ear as Gabby reported the broken window. She wondered if someone had been inside her home or, even worse, if someone might still be in there. Her teeth chattered and Gabby nudged up the heat. Gabby was still on the phone, but Emily kept her eyes glued to her front door. The longer she thought about it, the more certain she was of the identity of the window-breaker. Barnes heard her outside his house. He clearly had something to hide, and he wanted to frighten Emily away. He had ample time to drive over here, shatter her window, and hightail it back home before she and Gabby got back from getting ice cream.

A siren interrupted her train of thoughts. Gabby and Emily remained in the minivan, rolling down the window to speak to—who else?—Detective Gangly-Arms. He retrieved the keys from Emily and sent a couple of uniformed officers on ahead to search the house.

"You're keeping us awfully busy, Ms. Taylor. You either have some of the worst luck I've ever seen, or you have some mighty ticked-off enemies."

"It would appear so," Emily answered him drily, not wanting to show how truly frightened she was.

"Where were you when this happened?" Gangly-Arms asked her, his sweeping gesture toward her front window making it clear what "this" he was referring to.

Gabby leaned over, practically sprawling across Emily's lap. "We went for some ice cream and a little gossip. That's all, Detective Welks." Emily wasn't sure, but she thought Gabby might have even batted her eyelashes. Gabby oozed a certain sweetness and charm that could bring even the biggest fella to his knees. It would seem Gangly-Arms was not impervious to her feminine wiles. Even in the dim glow of the revolving police lights and the lamplight spilling onto the lawn through her shattered window, Emily noticed Gangly-Arm's blush. She almost felt sorry for this poor wet-behind-the-ears detective. He might have a shiny new badge and a well-honed instinct for investigation, but it would appear he still had a lot to learn about women.

"Of course." He stared into Gabby's large brown eyes, and she gave him a slow, smoldering smile. One of the officers approached and tapped him on the shoulder. Gangly-Arms startled like a kid caught popping his bubblegum in class. When he turned to address the officer, Emily whispered in Gabby's ear, "You should be ashamed of yourself, Gabriella Marie. What would Greg say?"

Gabby laughed softly and straightened up in her seat. "How do you think I handle Greg when he's upset?"

Emily scoffed because she knew better than that. Gabby was just trying to lighten the mood. Greg might think the sun rose and set in Gabby's eyes, but she was also convinced that Greg walked on water. They adored each other, and Emily prayed she would find a love like that of her own one day.

When Gangly-Arms turned back to them, he was all business. "Ms. Taylor, we need you to come inside and ascertain for us if anything is missing. Nothing appears to be disturbed, but we need to be sure."

Emily nodded woodenly, opened the minivan door, and headed back up her walk. Gabby hurried up beside her and grabbed her hand. She was grateful for the moral support, unsure of what she'd find inside. She expected the worst, so she was pleasantly surprised when the only disturbance was the small pile of leaves coloring her beige carpet. She took a quick tour of the rest of her duplex, but she didn't find anything amiss.

Returning to the living room, she was surprised to see that Tad had arrived and was deep in conversation with the detective. She whipped her head to send an accusatory glare Gabby's way, but her friend wouldn't meet her eyes. Leave it to Gabby to call in her form of the cavalry, she thought in defeat.

Gangly-Arms waved her over. After assuring him that nothing was missing, she stared uncomprehendingly at the object he held out to her.

"It's a brick." Was she slow tonight, or what?

But he was patient. "Yes. It would appear someone tossed this through your window. This note was wrapped around it." He held up a large plastic bag containing a typewritten note. It read: "Keep your nose out of things that are none of your business—OR ELSE!"

Emily was back to shivering uncontrollably. Tad and Gabby put an arm around her, one on each side. The detective asked quietly, "Do you have any idea who might have left you this message?"

Emily shook her head no, but of course, she was confident she knew exactly who wanted to scare or warn her away. She couldn't point a finger at Barnes, however, without telling Gangly-Arms where she and Gabby had been tonight. She was certain that neither the detective nor Tad would be amused by their nighttime trespassing expedition.

"I would say it was the same person who ran them off the road." Tad was visibly irritated. "Any leads there?"

"Not so far, Mr. Higginbotham, but I can assure you that this is an ongoing investigation. We'll test the brick and paper for fingerprints, and we'll try to trace this paper, but..." He didn't need to finish his sentence. They all knew it was a long shot. Whoever was behind all of this was smart and careful. The paper was generic white printer paper that could have been purchased anywhere. Emily knew this scare tactic had to be executed in a hurry, and in a rage if Barnes was behind it. And she was sure he was. Could she picture him running her and Gabby off the road and then acting as cool as the fall night to her face at school? Yes. Yes, she thought she could.

A new thought occurred to Emily. "Why do you think Jim changed his last name?" she asked the detective. "This all has to be tied back to him somehow, doesn't it?"

Gangly-Arms considered her question. "Let's not get too far ahead of ourselves," he finally said. "I take it you also have discovered who Jim really was?"

Emily nodded. "My mom remembered hearing the story at the time the kidnapping happened. She just called me a little while ago." She gave an *I'll tell you later* wave at Tad as he was clearly looking at her for an explanation as to what was going on.

Gangly-Arms continued. "I see. Well, we have learned that Jim Olsen was documented as telling the press that he would never rest until he found his nephew."

"But how does that tie him to Helen?" Emily asked. "She doesn't have any children."

"As I said, the investigation is ongoing."

Emily puzzled how Barnes was tied to all of this, too. There had to be a missing link that joined Jim, Helen, and Barnes together. She just hadn't found it. Yet.

She noticed that Gangly-Arms was watching her closely, so she gave him a bland smile. He frowned as he said, "I don't think I need to remind you again, Ms. Taylor, Mrs. Spencer…" He briefly met Gabby's eyes, and she gave him a blinding smile. He blushed again, and Emily felt Tad suppressing a laugh behind her. She pinched Gabby's arm, but the femme fatale only turned her wide eyed, innocent look on her. The poor detective cleared his throat. "As I was saying," he continued, the frown firmly back in place, "I'm sure I don't need to remind you to stay out of this investigation. We have things firmly under control."

"Of course, Detective," Gabby purred, subtly steering him toward the door.

He called back over his shoulder, "I'll be in touch." The door closed behind the last officer, and Emily collapsed on the sofa with a moan and put her head in her hands.

"Now what?" she asked, peeking between the fingers of her left hand. She didn't know how many more surprises she could handle.

"Now, I get home before Greg sends out a search party. Tad, take care of our girl." She made a "call me" gesture behind Tad's back, and then she was gone. Traitor.

"Pack your things," Tad told her and headed out the front door.

When she hadn't moved when he walked back in hefting a toolbox, he barked, "Why aren't you getting your stuff together?"

"More to the point, why would I be? And what are you doing with that?" She flung a hand toward the toolbox. She knew she sounded peevish, but she didn't care. This had been one long night, and she was in no mood to be bossed around by another irritable male.

Tad clenched and unclenched his fists, making a visible effort to calm down. "When Gabby told me what happened, I brought some supplies. I do live above a hardware store, you know. And you can't honestly think I'd let you stay here by yourself tonight?"

Emily thought about arguing on principle, but then she wondered if Barnes, or whoever threw the brick through her window, might make a return visit. Without a word, she pushed to her feet and went to the hall closet to pull out a small suitcase.

Satisfied, Tad went back out to retrieve a board to cover the shattered window. Emily tossed necessities haphazardly into her suitcase. Listening to the pounding of nails in her living room, Emily stared at her reflection in the mirror over the bathroom sink. Her face was pale and pinched, and her eyes looked too big for her face. She briefly debated calling her parents, but noting how late it was, she decided that call could wait until tomorrow. No need to worry them unnecessarily. There was nothing they could do anyway. So it looked like she would be staying the night at Tad's. The thought should have set her nerves to buzzing, but she was too exhausted to spare any excess emotion. She dragged her suitcase into the living room as Tad closed up his toolbox. "Ready to go?" he asked curtly. Emily didn't know what he had to be so grumpy about—it wasn't his window that had been broken.

Still, as she locked up, wondering if it was a futile effort, she said, "I'm sorry Gabby dragged you into this. I hope I didn't interrupt your Mathletes' practice."

Rather than answer her, Tad jerked her suitcase out of her hand and tossed it in the backseat. He barely waited until Emily had buckled her seat belt before tearing out of her driveway. Emily saw the set of his jaw in the intermittent illumination of street lamps. She could practically feel the waves of anger and frustration pouring off of him. Too tired to try and figure out Tad's moods tonight, she leaned back against the seat rest and closed her eyes. When Tad pulled to a stop with a jerk, she contemplated just sleeping in the car. She was too tired to move. She remained still, her eyes closed, but the intensity of Tad's stare seared her eyelids. Still not opening them, she said, "What's your problem anyway? I said I'm sorry you were drug into this. You could have just taken me to my parents."

"And given them another scare in the middle of the night? No, thank you. Having to tell them you were in the hospital due to a car accident is one of the worst things I've ever had to do." Emily was instantly contrite. She should have realized what a toll making that call must have taken on Tad. Of course he didn't want to scare her parents again. Neither did she. Emily felt choked by the onslaught of guilt.

"I'm sorry. I didn't mean to ruin your night again." She turned toward Tad, wide awake now, but to her surprise, he grabbed her suitcase, slammed out of the car, and stomped up the stairs to his apartment. Emily hurried to catch up. Tad unlocked the door and tossed her suitcase inside. Emily had never seen him this angry.

"Is that what you think I'm upset about? That Gabby interrupted our Mathletes' meeting?"

Emily cringed. So they *had* interrupted the meeting. "I know you're getting ready for a big meet. I'm really sorry. If—"

Tad cut her off with a shout, "Quit saying you're sorry!"

Emily was too stunned by Tad's outburst to even move. Tad was on a roll now and didn't even notice her silence. "I'm mad because you can't keep your nose out of things. I'm mad because I keep getting these phone calls about you that scare me half to death. I'm mad that you're messing around in a murder investigation like you actually know what you're doing!"

Emily's vision went red. Now, she too was irritated. "Don't know what I'm doing? Messing around? Who appointed you my guardian? I'm sorry for the calls, but I do *not* answer to you. I make my own decisions, and I take my own actions."

"You sure do," Tad steamed. "And a great job you're doing of it, too."

Emily stepped forward until she and Tad were practically nose to nose. Her voice was eerily quiet. "You're out of line, Tad."

If Tad hadn't been huffing and snorting like a bull about to charge, the change in her voice would have clued him in to just how angry Emily was at that moment. Instead, he said, "I'm not out of line. You are. You have to butt out of this whole mess."

"Listen here," she began, drilling a finger into his chest.

"No, you listen," he interrupted, grabbing her by the shoulders. Then he did the one thing Emily could never have seen coming. With one rough jerk, he knocked her off balance so that she stumbled into his chest, her cast catching him in the stomach. He didn't notice, though, because he was too busy taking her mouth in a kiss so full of heat she was sure the fire detectors would go off. When the initial shock wore off, she grabbed a fistful of his shirt and kissed him back. She had known that kissing Tad would be amazing, but she hadn't expected to feel a zing all the way down to her toes. And then she was left teetering as he let go of her shoulders as abruptly as he had grabbed them.

They stood a few feet apart, eyes locked, breath coming fast. For the first time that she could ever recall, Emily was speechless. Her mind was a complete blank for a span of several seconds, but when her brain engaged again, the voice in her head was talking so fast it sounded like a chipmunk on speed. *What did that kiss mean? Was it just a reaction to all the emotional upheaval surrounding them? Was Tad truly interested in her as more than a friend? What was he thinking now? Did he regret his impulsive move? Would he kiss her again?*

She worked up the nerve to ask him one of the million questions hammering at her, but before she could form the words, Tad turned and moved to the refrigerator. He grabbed a soda for himself and shoved another across the counter to her. The moment was lost. Emily drank deep of the sweet, icy soda to mask her disappointment. As the fizzy bubbles danced on her tongue, washing away the taste of Tad's kiss, she decided it was for the best. She was too emotionally fragile to deal with such an explosive issue tonight. She gave the air a sniff for any signs of smoke, but it would appear they had not actually set anything on fire. She slumped onto a barstool and uttered the first thing, unrelated to their steaming kiss, that popped into her head. "Could Jim's girlfriend, Stephanie, have a son?"

Tad took her non sequitur in stride. "Stephanie from the gym?" he clarified. She nodded and Tad came around to sit on a barstool next to her. "I assume you're asking because you think that child could be Jim's long-lost nephew." Again, she nodded. "But," he continued, "I don't think that scenario is plausible. Stephanie can't be more than thirty. That would make her only thirteen when Jim's nephew was born."

"I don't think she's involved anyway," Emily conceded. "My money's still on Barnes. Even if Gabby and I didn't find any—" She cut herself off before she let news of her and Gabby's nocturnal visit slip.

Her words were not lost on Tad. He gave her an arch look. "I'm not even going to ask where you and Gabby were sticking your noses tonight. But if you're that set on Barnes as a murderer, you need to exercise even more caution. He has access to you every day."

"Don't remind me," she muttered.

Tad ran a hand down her arm and her fingers tingled. She held her breath, waiting to see what Tad would do next. But his next words dashed any hope of a repeat performance of that smoldering kiss. "Speaking of seeing Barnes, tomorrow will be here before we know it. We'd better try to get some shut-eye." Tad retrieved her suitcase from where he'd tossed it earlier and carried it down the hall to the guest room.

"Thank you," she said, feeling suddenly shy around him.

"My pleasure." His tone was husky, and with a small smile, which she hoped was a little regretful, he turned and left, shutting the door behind him. Emily stood stock still, half hoping he'd come back. Then her rational side kicked in, and she fell back on the bed, fully clothed. Now was definitely not the time to explore the meaning behind that kiss. There was a murderer on the loose, Helen was still missing, and someone was targeting her. First things first. Still, as she tossed and turned throughout the night, despite the comfortable bed, Emily could hear Tad doing the same across the hall. She couldn't help but wonder if his mind was on Jim's murder and the ensuing trouble, or on that kiss and what it meant for their future relationship. It was one of the longest nights of Emily's life.

CHAPTER FOURTEEN

———

Emily breathed a sigh of relief as she slid out of Tad's car at school the next morning. They had tiptoed around each other all morning, never making eye contact, studiously avoiding any conversation that didn't revolve around the weather. Emily half expected to find her normally stick-straight hair either standing on end or as curly as Gabby's, with all the electricity crackling between them on the car ride to school. Glancing at her reflection in the door as she breezed through, she could see no visible signs of agitation, in her hair or otherwise. It looked like she was going to have to confront the situation with Tad at one point or another. They couldn't go on like this. She held a conversation with Tad in her head as she swung around the corner in the main office to check her mailbox. Even the make-believe conversation was awkward, so she wasn't paying attention to where she was going. She walked straight into Mr. Barnes, who was going the opposite direction. Emily leaped back like she'd been bitten by a snake. Barnes dropped his eyes and stormed past her, the hand clutching his mail white-knuckled, with either embarrassment or rage. Either way, Emily had no doubt that Barnes had definitely seen and/or heard her outside his house last night.

She contemplated this dilemma on the way up the stairs to her classroom. She hated to admit it, but she was frightened of Barnes. She truly believed he could be Jim's murderer. If only Helen would turn up! She hadn't seen any signs of a hostage while skulking around Barnes's house. But still…

There was no getting around it—she was going to have to tell Tad about her and Gabby's visit to Barnes's last night. She considered and discarded several different ways to break the information without Tad blowing up, which kept her mind occupied during morning classes. Thankfully, a large part of each hour was filled with a showing of some clips from the 1997 *Odyssey* miniseries with Armand Assante as Odysseus. She was prepping the students not only for a reading of Homer's *Odyssey*, but also for a writing assignment that would detail their own personal odysseys. All of the students seemed excited as they discussed the various clips shown, and Emily felt the success of seeing true interest glowing in her students' eyes.

As soon as her conference hour rolled around, however, she steeled her spine and headed over to Tad's classroom. She took the precaution of shutting the door behind her in case he reacted as she highly suspected he would. Tad stopped grading papers and listened closely as she detailed the what, when, and why of her and Gabby's spying expedition. Emily could hear Tad grinding his teeth, but he remained calm. When she had finished, she chewed on the edge of an already-ravaged fingernail, waiting for his pronouncement on her stupidity. Instead, he cleared his throat and asked quietly, like a man trying not to shout, "Are you scared, Emily? Is this something we should take to the police?"

Emily's pride flew out the window, and she confessed to feeling truly terrified of Barnes now. "Still, we can't go to the police because we have nothing but suspicious feelings. Trust me, I've considered it, but I don't think the police have taken up the practice of arresting people for being despicable."

Tad tapped his red grading pen as he considered. Emily hated that pen. She had never graded in red because no student was ever encouraged by finding his or her paper bleeding with critiques. Now the color also reminded her of that terrifying moment when she had discovered Jim. Tad interrupted her morbid thoughts. "Okay, then, we need to find some concrete facts. You said you did some research into Barnes's past, but all you found was the allegation from the girl of inappropriate conduct, right?" When Emily nodded, he continued. "So we dig some more."

They hunkered down behind his desk, but the list of sites that filled Tad's screen were the same ones Emily had read and discarded as unimportant the other day. "We have to narrow the search further," Tad said as he confined the search to Richard Barneses in Missouri. Still, their search was unproductive. Tad got up to pace, and Emily watched him, at a loss for ideas. Suddenly, Tad whirled back to the computer and started a new search. His eyes were full of excitement as he turned to her. "His car!" he exclaimed.

"What about it?" Emily asked. "I mean, we could look up the VIN number or the dealer he purchased it from, but what would that tell us about his past?"

"No. His car itself," Tad corrected. At her blank look, he prodded, "His license plate?"

"I give up. I know nothing about cars, and I have no idea what you're talking about."

Tad shoved at his hair. He really needed a haircut, but Emily found the lock of hair that fell over his forehead oddly endearing. "He has one of those vanity plates. Didn't you notice?"

"No," Emily admitted. "I didn't pay that close of attention. But how will that help us narrow our search?"

"We can use his middle initial." Tad looked like an eager puppy, and Emily found her heart melting a bit more. She ignored the feeling and tried to picture Barnes's license plate instead. Nothing came to mind.

"I think it says something like R-Man. I can't remember the first part," Tad said.

"I'll look through the teachers' lounge window. You can see the parking lot from there."

"Perfect," Tad beamed.

Emily checked the hallway. It was clear, so she made a mad dash across the hall to the lounge. The *Mission Impossible* theme song played in her head as she flattened herself against the wall next to the window and peered around. The window was foggy. Laughing at her own James Bond-like behavior, Emily swiped at the window and squinted, trying to make out the letters on the Cobra's license plate. She could clearly see the *R*, and the third letter was *B*, but the middle letter could be an *L* or an *F* or an *E*.

Straining her eyes, she was distracted by a movement between two of the other cars in the lot. A man in a black trench coat and a navy baseball cap was moving slowly. Something about him seemed familiar, and when he looked up to scan the row of windows at the back of the building, Emily had a clear view of his face. She gasped. It was the same man she had seen sneaking away from Jim's funeral!

Emily spun toward the door. Glancing at Tad's classroom, she debated stopping to tell him what she was doing, but there was no time. She careened down the back staircase, bursting out the back doors. She sprinted to the spot where the man had been standing moments ago, but he was nowhere to be seen. The man moved like a bat. Frustrated, she headed back toward the school doors. As she passed Barnes's car, however, she stopped to get a clear look at his license plate. Now she could see that it read "REB-MAN." She snorted. "Man," her foot. The "man" was a toad all the way.

Halfway back up the stairs, she ran into Tad. "Where did you go?" He looked bewildered. For the second time in the space of an hour, Emily admitted to her reckless behavior. "He disappeared into thin air, just like before," she huffed.

"Do *not* do that again," Tad told her firmly and headed back to his classroom. Emily bit her tongue to keep from sticking it out at his retreating back. Mature, she knew, but as much as she wanted to see where this thing, if there even was a thing, was going between her and Tad, she didn't need a keeper. She could take care of herself just fine, thank you very much. Except for her broken arm. And her broken window. Oh, and her lack of wheels…whatever.

Trailing behind Tad, Emily remembered she had seen Barnes's license plate. She relayed the information to Tad, and he scooted behind his desk to narrow his search further. They spent the rest of their shared conference hour skimming through several pages of uninformative articles. Tad pushed away from the computer with frustration. Emily continued to stare at the screen, desperately trying to come up with another way to get some proof that Barnes was a dangerous criminal. The last hit on the results screen caught her eye, and she laughed. It was a picture of a Harlequin Romance. She pointed it out to Tad, joking that she highly doubted he was the lead character in a woman's romance novel.

"Why did that come up in our search?" Tad wondered aloud, clicking the link. The page that came up was an article on best-selling Harlequin Romance writer Carrie Brannon. Emily shrugged and turned away.

"Doesn't seem to have anything to do with Barnes. I guess I'd better go get ready for my afternoon classes." She was almost to the door when Tad let out a hoot of laughter.

"You have to see this, Em." Tad's laughter shook his shoulders. He pointed to the last line of the article.

Emily leaned over him to read aloud, "Readers might be interested to know that Carrie Brannon is the pen name for Richard E. Barnes, school teacher by day, romance writer by night."

Emily dropped into the nearest chair, staring at Tad in disbelief. "A romance writer? Barnes? Please tell me this is a sick joke."

Tad continued to snicker as he pointed out, "It all makes sense. That's where he got the money for that car. It's probably also why he's so secretive. I highly doubt he'd want this information to get around. The students would have a heyday with it. He'd be the laughingstock of Ellington, no matter how much money he makes writing."

Emily fumed. Barnes? Life was so unfair. She was the English teacher with a creative writing minor. She was the one who dreamt of writing a best-selling novel one day. Barnes? Dang it all, there was no way he could be the bad guy in all of this if *this* was the secret he was covering up.

Tad read her mind. "Guess this puts Barnes at the bottom of the suspect list, huh? He'd have no reason to blackmail anyone. If anything, it would be the other way around."

"I guess so," Emily grumped. This was certainly an unexpected, and unwelcome, revelation.

She hated to ask it, but she had to. "You don't think Helen could have been blackmailing him, do you? She had to need the money, and clearly, Barnes has it."

"Then why was Jim the one murdered? And that still doesn't explain anything about his missing nephew."

"True," Emily agreed.

Before the bell rang and they both had to get back to work, she and Tad looked up the article on the missing Olsen child. It was a heartrending story. A young, wealthy couple, both on the rise in their law careers, had a baby boy. The mother was suffering from severe postpartum depression. In a move he hoped would help her, her husband, Stephen Olsen, hired a nanny, Bridget McMillan, to help care for their son. The nanny had taken him out to the park one day so that the young, overwhelmed mother could take a nap. A little girl had fallen off the swings and the nanny went over to help her up. When she turned back to the baby carriage, the baby was gone. The police searched and searched. At first, the nanny was suspected, but once the police cleared her, she moved away, apparently devastated by the kidnapping of the child on her watch. The parents were overcome with grief, offering all kinds of rewards for any information concerning the missing child. Jim Olsen, the younger brother of the father, became a spokesman for the family. He swore that he would not rest until his nephew was found.

In a follow-up to the article, Tad and Emily silently read about the suicide of the young mother. It was a tragic story. Years passed, and the father gave up hope of ever recovering his lost child. His world had been too completely shattered. Jim, however, had never given up the search.

"Wow," Emily whispered. "Who would have known Jim was hiding such a past?"

"Goes to show you never know what's going on in someone else's life behind closed doors. No matter how much of an open book they may seem," Tad said, echoing Gabby's sentiments the night of their stakeout.

Emily began to cry softly, once again filled with grief at the death of a good man, a kind man. Tad wrapped her in his arms, letting her cry. Emily dimly thought, *This is becoming a pattern.* She pulled back, looking into Tad's eyes. She saw a matching grief there. Wanting to soothe him and herself, she closed her eyes and leaned forward, and—the bell rang. They sprang apart like they'd been shocked with a cattle prod. Emily ducked her head, appalled that she had been about to kiss Tad right here in the middle of a school day. Without looking back, she hurried to her own classroom to get on with her day.

* * *

Emily ate lunch in her classroom, hoping to avoid both Barnes and Tad. She tapped out a new list of questions they still needed to answer:

1. Was Jim murdered because he was on the trail of his nephew?

2. Who did Jim meet with at the high school that night?

3. Was Stephanie involved? She had an inkling of Jim's past...

4. WHERE WAS HELEN? Was her disappearance tied to Jim's death, or was it something else entirely?

5. Who ran Gabby and me off the road? Who threw the brick through my window? Was it the same person?

Emily read over the list and tried to make connections between the questions. If all this was tied to Jim's nephew, did that mean the boy was here in Ellington? The true implications of that sunk in, and Emily found herself staring at the list of names in her grade book, wondering if one of the boys listed there could be the missing Olsen child. It seemed like quite a stretch, though, as she knew the parents of 99 percent of her students. She wanted to run her new idea by Tad, but the bell was ringing. It would have to wait until after school.

* * *

As afternoon classes got under way, Emily was anxious to see how Stevie would react to the movie clips. She hoped that writing about his own odyssey would draw him out, giving him a chance to express his feelings about all the moves he and his mom had made. True to his word, he had been putting more effort into class. Small victories like this made teaching worthwhile, in Emily's opinion.

To her disappointment, though, Stevie wasn't in class. None of the students had any idea where he was. A couple of the football players said he hadn't been at practice the night before. Since she hadn't gotten a note for homework to be sent to the office, Emily was curious where he was. As soon as the final bell rang, she went down to the office to inquire what Arlene had said when she phoned in Stevie's absence that morning. The secretary double-checked her pile of notices twice, but Arlene had never called. Emily thanked her and headed back up to her classroom.

She tried to do some grading to pass the time until Tad was done with his Mathletes' practice, but she couldn't concentrate. An unsettled feeling was roiling in her belly, and she was too restless to sit still. The fact that Arlene hadn't called in to report Stevie's absence seemed uncharacteristic. She came across as the type of person who was always on top of things. She wouldn't want Stevie to have an unexcused absence on his record.

Emily began straightening her desk for something to do since she couldn't concentrate on grading. Shuffling a stack of mythology notes to one side, a Maxine Post-it Note fluttered to the floor. Emily picked it up and saw it was the contact information she had written down for Arlene Davis. Emily recalled Arlene's serious face and anxiousness to help her son in any possible way. But then she pictured Stevie, hair in his eyes, a hangdog expression on his face. True, he had promised her that he would do better in class, and he had been trying, but she couldn't forget the lost look he had given her when he said he was sick of moving. An idea struck Emily—could Stevie have finally decided to rebel against his mother? Did he cut class today? Or even worse, had he run away? Before she could second-guess herself, Emily scooped up her cell and dialed Stevie's home number. It rang and rang, but no one picked up, and the answering machine never kicked on.

The uneasiness she had been feeling grew to the point that she felt physically ill. She thought about interrupting Tad and telling him her worries, but she was sure he would think she was being hysterical. And maybe she was. But the fact remained that this all seemed out of character. She had to talk to Arlene to make sure Stevie was okay, but on the off chance he wasn't, she didn't want to alarm Arlene unnecessarily. It would be better to have this conversation in person.

Her worry building, Emily thought of Helen's disappearance. Could Stevie be in the same situation as Helen? There were too many frightening scenarios to consider. She had to focus on one thing at time. Stevie might very well be at home, too sick to answer the phone. The best way to find out for sure would be to talk to Arlene. She scooped up her purse and headed out the door. Halfway to the stairs she remembered she was lacking transportation. She stomped her foot in frustration. If she ever got her hands on the person who ran Gabby and her off the road, she'd throttle them. She missed her PT as much as if it had been a real live person.

After a quick internal debate, she decided not to interrupt Tad's Mathletes' practice again. He would be tied up for at least another hour, so she had plenty of time to borrow his Prius and dash over to Masterson Real Estate to talk to Arlene. They would probably have a laugh over her ridiculous imagination, and then she could be back before Tad even knew she was gone. In her years of teaching, she had learned it was better to ask for forgiveness instead of permission, and if things went well, she wouldn't have to ask for either.

Tad had left his classroom door unlocked, per usual, so she slipped inside without turning on the light. No need to draw attention to the fact that someone was in his room when he was busy with the Mathletes. Emily silently slid open the top, right-hand drawer of his desk. He kept a carved wooden box in there that a student had given him as a thank you gift his first year of teaching. That student had gone on to be a math teacher himself, and that box had become one of Tad's most prized possessions. He normally kept his keys and some loose change in the box. Emily prayed that he had not changed his ways. Lifting the wooden lid, she let out a whoosh of relief. Thank goodness—Tad was predictable even when nothing else in the world was. She grabbed the keys to his Prius and sent him a silent apology. Tad would never knowingly allow her to drive his precious car. But since she would be back before he could even notice she'd borrowed the Prius, what he didn't know wouldn't hurt him.

CHAPTER FIFTEEN

A sharply dressed man in a gray suit and a red power tie hopped up to greet Emily as she pushed through the front door of Masterson Real Estate. His rectangular, gold name tag read "Gil," she noticed as he flashed her a *trust me and I'll sell you your dream house* smile. Repulsed by his slightly desperate air, Emily took some small satisfaction in asking for Arlene Davis in response to his query of how he could help. Gil's trust-me smile momentarily disappeared as he emitted an unprofessional snort, but then a predatory shark smile, all teeth, spread across his face as he smelled new blood in the waters. "Unfortunately, Ms...." He waited for her to fill in the gap, but Emily remained silent, returning his toothy grin. Gil shrugged and continued. "Arlene abruptly quit this morning."

"What?" Emily was startled into asking. She understood the words—she just couldn't fathom the meaning behind them. "Why?"

Gil attempted to pull off a sympathetic look, but Emily wasn't buying it. "Something about her son being unhappy at Ellington High. Her world revolves around that kid, I swear. Anyway, she said as how she'd already found a new job, she planned to leave immediately. If you were working with her, I'd be happy to help you. I've taken over her listings, and—" Gil continued his spiel even as she turned and pushed blindly back out onto the sidewalk.

Arlene had quit? Leaving immediately? She knew Stevie was upset about Coach Layton, but he'd been making strides in her class lately. He also appeared to have several new friends. Had she been too concerned with Helen's disappearance to see how miserable Stevie really was?

Glancing in the rearview mirror as she prepared to back the Prius out of its parking place, she spotted a dark-haired figure moving quickly down the sidewalk, chin tucked down into the collar of his jacket. Emily slammed on the brakes and watched as the man headed to a black Lincoln Navigator parked on the opposite side of the street. A dark SUV? Heart pounding, Emily threw the Prius in reverse and headed toward the parked car. As she passed the man, he was climbing into the driver's seat, and she got a clear look at his face. It was the same man she'd seen at Jim's funeral, and later, outside the school. Could he be following her? And that vehicle—could it be the same one that ran her and Gabby off the road? The Navigator looked brand new to her, but as Gabby had pointed out, there *had* been enough time to have any damage fixed by now.

Emily accelerated, avoiding meeting the man's eyes. Still, his face loomed before her, once again oddly familiar looking. As Emily turned onto the street that would lead her back to the school, she had a sudden recollection of Jim, larger than life, telling some ridiculous joke to Tad about how you could go to a concert for forty-five cents. When Tad had asked him how, Jim had set his face in serious lines and said, "You go to see 50 Cent, followed by Nickelback." Emily had read that same joke on Pinterest, but it wasn't the corny punch line that was bothering her now. It was Jim's face when he put on that serious look. It was the exact same look she had seen just now on the face of the man climbing into the Lincoln Navigator.

A horn blared behind her, and Emily gave the steering wheel a hard jerk to the right. Deep in thought, she had swerved over the center line, paying more attention to her new revelation than to her driving. She pulled into the teachers' lot and marveled at the discovery. It made perfect sense! The man had been at Jim's funeral because he was Jim's older brother, Stephen Olsen.

Focusing on his image in her mind, Emily could see that the man in the Navigator did clearly look like an older version of Jim. Detective Gangly-Arms had said there had been some difficulty in locating Jim's brother. He had been presumed to still be in New York. But now it looked like he'd been here in Ellington the whole time. But why hadn't he come forward and introduced himself? And furthermore, why was he still here? Did this have anything to do with his missing son? Was she right before? Was the missing Olsen baby one of the students currently in attendance at Ellington High?

The idea boggled the mind. If the strange man was Stephen Olsen and he was here for his son, then that meant Jim had probably located his nephew but been killed before he could do anything about it. Chances were high he had been watching the boy for a while, trying to find concrete evidence of his true identity. So why had he been killed *now*? And what about Helen? As the counselor, she had access to a lot of privileged information. Had she also discovered that the missing Olsen child was attending Ellington High? Had she known Jim's secret identity as the boy's uncle? Barnes had said he overheard them arguing about something and that they had mentioned the police. It galled Emily to admit the snake had actually not been a deceitful serpent this time.

Drumming the fingers of her good hand on the steering wheel, Emily continued to run through various scenarios in her mind. Why would Helen and Jim have been arguing? Did Helen disappear because she was guilty of murdering Jim? Maybe they had been arguing, and it was all a heat-of-the-moment type of thing. Maybe Helen had been acting in self-defense. Or, worse yet, maybe Helen was the person Jim was meeting that night, but the killer got there first. But if that was the case, wouldn't Helen have discovered Jim's body and called the police? Or would the killer have waited and gotten rid of Helen too? Helen's body had not been found, but maybe that was because the police were only looking in obvious places, assuming she was alive and well. Another frightening scenario presented itself. What if Helen had discovered Jim's body, heard someone leaving, and followed and confronted that person? That sounded like the type of fearless thing Helen would do. Maybe whoever had killed Jim had then killed Helen, and if so, her body might be anywhere. Emily trembled, overcome with fear for her friend. She knew in her heart of hearts that Helen was innocent. That meant she could only hope and pray that Helen was still alive. Somewhere.

She needed to talk to Stephen Olsen. Maybe he knew something that was preventing him from coming forward. Emily pointed the car back in the direction she'd come. Mathletes' practice wasn't over yet, and with any luck, she'd be able to find the black Navigator quickly. There weren't too many of those roaming the streets of Ellington.

When Emily passed back by Masterson Real Estate, she saw Gil pacing in front of the door. The ball of dread in her stomach grew. Arlene quitting so abruptly, and then Stevie not being at school, was very odd. Surely Arlene would have come up to the school to withdraw Stevie. Yet the school hadn't heard a thing.

Her dread grew with every mile she drove. She thought about how Stevie had been adamant that Helen was innocent. He had also been close to Jim. Stevie was too young to remember anything about the Olsen case, but what if he had overheard something? Stevie was a bright kid. Had Stevie disappeared the same way Helen had? Did they both know too much? Emily pictured Arlene busily packing, completely unaware that Stevie hadn't been to school that day. She was thoroughly convinced that Arlene kept close tabs on Stevie, and if he had willingly not been at school, she would have called. However, if Stevie had never made it to school…

The thought was too horrible to finish.

Emily still wanted to locate Stephen Olsen, but right now she decided she needed to check on Stevie more. She tried Arlene's cell again. The call went straight to voice mail, but Emily chose not to leave a message, afraid she wouldn't be able to keep the fear out of her voice. Her brain told her there was a good chance that Stevie was fine and Arlene was just too busy packing to call or remember to have Stevie do it. Her heart, however, knew that the great bard had been right—something was rotten in the state of Denmark. An inexplicable sense of urgency propelled her toward the outskirts of town, her search for the black Navigator put on hold.

Arlene had bought the old Covell homestead when she and Stevie moved to Ellington the past summer. The Covells had been anxious to sell. They had finally retired and were headed for a life of rest and relaxation in Florida. Her mom had told her that Arlene had gotten the place for a song. The house itself was old, but it had been lovingly maintained. Several people had wondered why a single mom would want to mess with all that land, but Emily figured she liked the privacy. The views around the old Covell place were beautiful, with stately, old trees and gently rolling hills. Arlene was renting the ground out to a neighbor who was farming it for her for some extra income. Emily thought Arlene had made an excellent investment. Why would she want to uproot Stevie's life yet again when she had such a beautiful place to live, as well as a great job?

The old homestead was about five miles outside of town off of Highway E. Emily took the turn off of the blacktop and onto the gravel road fast enough to have the back tires spinning. She forced herself to slow down so that she could see through the churned-up dust. The tin roof of the ancient red barn that perched on the ridge behind the house came into view. Emily turned into the winding drive, trying to maintain a sedate pace. Her eyes anxiously roved the area as she parked, but the place looked deserted, left to doze in the late afternoon sun. The blinds on all the front windows were tightly closed, and there wasn't a car in sight. Emily rang the bell, pounded on the door, and called out for Arlene, but there was no response. She stood undecidedly on the front porch steps, shading her eyes so she could scan for any sign of life. The only movement was a murder of crows settling down in a nearby field. Their flight was silent, a black smudge on the pale-blue sky. The whole world seemed to be holding its breath, anticipating the worst. A cloud drifted across the pale October sun, and the landscape turned into a set from an old noir film. Emily was determined not to let the old familiar scene play out, though. She would not be the naïve, helpless damsel in distress. Today the part of the fearless, clever heroine would be played by one Emily Taylor.

Determined to make sure the place was as deserted as it appeared to be, Emily made a circuit of the house, trying all the windows and doors. As she rounded the far corner, she could have sworn she heard a muffled scream, but then a strong gust of wind had the old, rusty windmill screeching in the silence. The sound set Emily's teeth on edge, stretching her nerves taut. Emily's step faltered, and for the first time, she began to wonder if coming out here by herself had been a good idea. Still, she'd come too far to give up now.

Since the house wasn't giving up any secrets, Emily turned to the outbuildings. The large barn doors were secured with a padlock that looked like it meant business. Next to the barn was an open-front machine shed, empty but for a mama cat, who had made a home for her babies in some leftover hay. Emily gave the protective mama a wide berth as she ducked between the buildings. A ramshackle, white shed lurked in the shadows behind the hulking machine shed. From its size, Emily figured the shed had once housed gardening tools, possibly even a lawnmower. The door was locked tight, but a cursory glance showed a round window set high in the back wall. Even on her tiptoes, Emily couldn't see over the sill. She returned to the machine shed and rummaged until she unearthed a crumbling cinder block. It was awkward to heft and haul with only one good arm, but she managed. The heels of her chocolate leather boots sank into earth softened by the recent rains as she positioned the cinder block under the window, turning it on its end to give her extra height. The wind had picked up and was tugging at the hem of her plaid skirt as she balanced on one foot, leaning into the shed's wall for balance. The cinder block provided just enough height for her to see into the shed. When she'd started on this search, Emily hadn't been sure what she was looking for. But that didn't change the fact that she knew it when she found it.

Inside the shed sat a familiar blue Tahoe. A round Scentsy hanger dangled from the rearview mirror. The vehicle had been pulled in straight rather than backed in, giving her an unobstructed view of its front. The passenger side showed signs of serious damage. The bumper had been torn loose, the headlight smashed, and the door mangled almost beyond recognition. Emily stared in slack-jawed horror at the streaks of red paint amid the wreckage.

Feeling suddenly lightheaded, Emily dropped back down to the ground, carefully lowering herself to sit on the cinder block. Her heart pounded and her fingers shook. The sun retreated behind a cloud once again, and Emily let loose a gurgle of hysterical laughter as she realized she was the damsel in distress after all. She felt as weak as the kittens in the machine shed. Her world teetered precariously on the brink of this discovery, for there was no denying it—this was the vehicle that had run her and Gabby off the road, sending them plummeting to probable death. But what made this discovery even worse was the second undeniable fact—this was Helen's vehicle. Emily's mind spewed nothing but gibberish. This was too much to take in. It was like facing a geometry problem, a subject that had baffled her in high school. She now had the proof, but she still had no answer.

Why was Helen's vehicle in Arlene's garage? Had Helen run them off the road? But no, that scenario didn't make sense unless she was in cahoots with Arlene, since the vehicle was on Arlene's property. And would Helen want to hurt her and Gabby, or Jim for that matter? And didn't she see that by running away and hiding, she had only made herself look guiltier? None of this made sense.

Pacing behind the shed, Emily thought back to the moment this nightmare had started. Jim's murder. Barnes had said that Helen and Jim had argued. But about what? Why did they mention the police? Unbidden, an image of Jim's face, eyes staring, muscles slack, popped into her mind. She fought her own instinct to push the image away and focused instead on why Jim's face seemed so crucial to her in helping figure out this mess. Slowly, Jim's face, with his large, dark eyes, ready smile, and crown of dark hair morphed into a serious face with intent eyes, staring up at her from the teachers' parking lot. Jim and Stephen Olsen. She had made that connection, but now the final image fell into the kaleidoscope. With a final twist of the dial, the truth tumbled clear. She had been staring at those same dark, intent eyes since school began. Or at least she had been when they weren't hiding behind a fringe of even darker hair. Jim had sworn that he would not rest until he found his nephew. And in Ellington, Jim had found him on his own football team. Stevie Davis was Jim's nephew, the Olsen baby kidnapped seventeen years earlier.

Racing to Tad's car and her cell phone, she tried to sort through the rest of it. Arlene—fiercely protective of her son, always on the move. Jim—a caring coach who found more than just a new player. Helen—a conscientious counselor who would want to follow the proper channels to confirm Stevie's true identity with the least amount of trauma to the withdrawn seventeen-year-old boy. Once Jim had discovered the truth, he must have confided in Helen, or vice versa. Jim was ready to go to the authorities. But that could never happen. Arlene must have gotten wind of Jim's plans. Arlene would do whatever she had to in order to ensure that she never lost her son.

CHAPTER SIXTEEN

———

Emily's breath came in wheezing gulps as she rummaged through her purse for her cell phone. Desperate now, she dumped the purse's contents on the passenger seat, diving onto her phone like a diet-starved person pounces on a piece of chocolate cake. Her fingers trembled as she punched in Tad's cell number. Signal was spotty back here in the hills, but she left a message anyway. He must still be in Mathletes' practice. Surely he would get the message when he discovered his car was missing. Not for the first time in her life, she regretted her impetuous behavior. Why hadn't she let someone know where she was going? She considered driving back to town and going to speak to Detective Gangly-Arms in person. But she was afraid that if she left, this crucial piece of evidence, Helen's Tahoe, might disappear. Arlene may have cleared out, but Emily knew she was too cautious to leave behind something so incriminating. Where was she now was the question. And when would she be back?

Emily got into the car and locked the doors, grabbing up her conspicuous pink camo pepper spray can for defense. She would have preferred her .38 Special, but Tad wasn't fond of guns, so she knew there was no chance she'd find a pistol stashed in a compartment of his car. Emily tried Detective Gangly-Arms, but he wasn't in. She left a message for him to call her immediately as she had some new evidence in the Jim Layton murder case. If she was lucky, Tad would get her message soon and head this way with the detective in tow. She checked her phone again for any messages she might have missed due to the poor signal strength, but, as usual, luck was not with her. Her phone emitted one traitorous beep before her Rainbow Brite background faded to black. Her battery was dead. She hadn't charged it last night because she had forgotten her wall charger as Tad was hustling her out of her duplex.

Wind buffeted the car and dark clouds now loomed on the horizon. Emily waffled between staying put and fleeing back to town. But as soon as she left, Helen's Tahoe would disappear, and Arlene would be gone in the wind. Helen! Emily couldn't believe her own stupidity. She knew that Stevie was safe now, because no matter how unhinged Arlene became, she would never hurt her "son." But where was Helen? Had Arlene already gotten rid of that loose end? Tears flooded her eyes, and she blinked furiously, clutching her pepper spray in a death grip. She struggled to think like a psychopathic killer. It actually wasn't as hard as she'd thought it would be. Scary. But other matters ranked higher on her scale of terror right now.

If Arlene had killed Helen, why hadn't they found her body? And if Helen was still alive, like Emily hoped and prayed, it had to be because Helen still served some purpose for Arlene. But what? And how did Helen get involved in this whole mess anyway?

A faint rumble of thunder rolled in with the darkening clouds. It had been thundering when she found Jim's body, too. While Emily didn't put much stock into reading the signs of the universe, the coincidence could not be ignored. An answering rumble deep within her convinced her that she needed to act quickly if this storm was going to end with a different fate.

The homestead was deserted, so where else could Helen be? Fat raindrops plopped on the windshield, creating small puddles before rolling down the glass like tears. Emily wracked her brain, trying to keep her own tears at bay. She didn't know Arlene well enough to know where her favorite haunts might be. Where could she hide a person? Did she rent a storage facility around here? Maybe someone at Masterson Real Estate could tell her. She picked up her phone and poked the button to wake it up. The screen remained dark. Remembering the dead battery, she tossed the useless phone aside. "That battery better be the only dead thing I find tonight." She spoke the words aloud, startling herself.

The rain was now a steady downpour, a good soaking rain, the farmers would call it. Dusk was encroaching on the last stubborn lights of day, decreasing visibility. Where was Tad? Or Detective Gangly-Arms? Or both? Tad had to be out of Mathletes' practice by now.

Emily turned the car back on for warmth. She tried to approach how to locate Helen from a logical standpoint. She wasn't at the school. She wasn't at her home. Arlene's place was deserted. Or was it? What if the sound she had heard earlier wasn't the windmill after all, but someone crying for help? She flipped on the car lights, clicking on the high beams. There were still no visible signs of life, so she had two choices. She could drive to town for help, wasting precious time and risking missing Tad and losing evidence, or she could go check out the house one more time to be safe. Option one was undoubtedly the safer of the two, but Emily was prone to jumping headlong into any option two, intent upon results. Anything had to be better than just sitting here, worrying about Helen and Stevie. Besides, Tad should be arriving with backup at any moment.

Tad had his umbrella with him, as Mr. Always-Prepared had heard there was a 30 percent chance for rain again today. Looked like it was a 100 percent chance that Emily was going to get soaked. Slamming the car door, she moved quickly, yet cautiously, through the sheet of rain to the shelter of the porch. It would be just like her to fall on the wet grass and break her ankle now, too.

The front door and windows were still locked tight. The original leaded-glass windows would be next to impossible to break, even if there was something handy to smash them with. Unfortunately, the porch was devoid of all furniture. Not even a stray flowerpot offered itself up as a battering ram. The faded welcome mat certainly wouldn't do her much good, and she doubted she could pick the lock even if she had the right tools, which, of course, she didn't. She didn't even have a bobby pin in her chestnut hair. Emily decided she had to be world's worst heroine-in-training.

She left the shelter of the porch and headed back around the house. She remembered a small back door on the east side of the house. The rain was coming down even harder, if that was possible. At this rate, she'd need a boat in order to rescue anyone. She cheered aloud when she saw the window, covered by a heavy curtain, in the top half of the back door. The cinder block would easily break the window, but it was too far away to haul to the back door. Emily willed herself to think despite the bone-numbing chill of the rain. Thankfully, the red woolen scarf she had pinned around her cast today was keeping it relatively dry. She hefted her right arm. Her cast was heavy enough to break the glass, but she didn't want to risk re-creating the healing break in her arm. The only option left was to use her fist. She yanked off the red scarf and wrapped it around her left hand. Her cast was now sopping wet, but at least the break in her arm was still protected.

Emily closed her eyes, took a deep breath, and channeled Dorothy L. Sayers's heroine Harriet Vane. She had once broken a window using this method. Emily opened her eyes and punched with all her might. What did she have to lose, other than a few liters of blood if she split open her wrist? But, to her surprise and satisfaction, the window now sported a jagged hole and her wrist was both uncut and intact. She carefully used her scarf-covered hand to tap out the loose, jagged pieces. Standing on her tiptoes (thank goodness for high heels!), she could get her arm far enough inside the window to turn the lock. Seconds later, she stood in the dim, but blessedly dry, kitchen of the old farmhouse. Stepping carefully over the broken glass, Emily listened intently. The only sounds were the rain drumming a tattoo on the roof and her own breaths rasping harshly in the still house. An older dinette set had an air of abandonment about it and was the only furniture in the kitchen and attached dining room. The fridge hummed, and the ice machine rattled as it dumped a new load of ice, the sound magnified in the empty room. Emily cracked the fridge door open, then yanked it wide, surprised to see that it was fully stocked. If Arlene was leaving town, she would have cleaned out the refrigerator so as to not arouse suspicion in Stevie. Either she was in too big of a hurry to worry about keeping up appearances, or she planned to come back later.

Emily threw open a few cupboards, but as she expected, they were bare. The pantry was also empty, except for a few moldy onions and a rusty mousetrap holding an anemic hunk of cheese. As she moved into the living room, she stumbled over a box, dropping her pepper spray, which rolled off into the hallway. The living room was shrouded in darkness due to the drawn curtains and raging storm. She twitched aside one of the curtains at the front window. Rain slashed down, but no headlights appeared. She turned and bumped her way down the hallway, but she couldn't find her pepper spray in the gloom. She gave up the search, hurrying to explore the rest of the house.

Two doors opened off the hallway to the left, both leading to empty rooms. A small powder room under the stairs was also uninhabited. The final room on the right side of the hall appeared to be the master bedroom. There was a small alcove holding an old-fashioned secretary desk. Emily flipped open the top, but only dust bunnies held court inside. Not even a stray receipt remained. The en suite bathroom held a couple of smaller sealed boxes, but the medicine cabinet and small linen closet gave no sign of ever having been in use.

Lighting flashed and thunder boomed. Emily took advantage of the temporary illumination to hurry to the staircase. Every step creaked, and by the time she reached the second floor, her nerves were stretched to the breaking point. Another two bedrooms were on the left side of the hallway. One still bore traces of sticky tack on the wall as if a poster had hung there recently. Emily deduced that this had been Stevie's room. The right side of the hall held a full bath and what might have been another bedroom or study. Nothing remained but a few tightly sealed boxes. Those boxes were ticking time bombs. Arlene might return for them at any moment, and this rescue mission of Emily's could blow up in her face.

So far, Emily had not turned on any lights or called out, for fear Arlene would return and be upon her before Emily heard her. The looming boxes, the relentless rain, and the panic that threatened to swamp her had Emily throwing caution to the winds. She began screaming Helen's and Stevie's names. She hadn't noticed an inside entrance to a cellar, but she figured there had to be attic access somewhere up here. Emily went back to each closet to check their ceilings, but she didn't find any opening.

Hoarse from repeated shouting, Emily paused to peek out of a front-facing window. Still no sign of anyone. She was losing hope of backup arriving. Despite her instinct that Helen,

Stevie, or both of them had to be somewhere in this house, she was ready to admit defeat. If she drove back to town now, she could get more people to help her search. She'd just have to take her chances that Arlene wouldn't come back while she was gone.

Emily headed back down the stairs, the creaking of the steps, the wet slap of her boots, and the rain creating its own symphony. When she reached the last step, however, the creaking continued. Emily held her breath and stood completely still at the base of the stairs. Could she be hearing the windmill screech from her place inside the house, even over the sound of the rain? Doubtful. She took a tentative step forward. The creaking continued. She desperately wished she was still holding on to her pepper spray. Had someone else entered the house?

Her heart in her throat, Emily took a quick peek outside. Tad's Prius remained the only vehicle in sight. Turning back to the hallway, she tried to determine the direction the sound was coming from. She called out Helen's and Stevie's names again. This time she heard a loud and distinctive thump coming from the master bedroom. Emily raced into the dark room, calling, "Who's there? Helen? Stevie?"

Darkness had filled the room so that she could barely make out the secretary in the alcove. She risked flipping on the overhead light, blinking rapidly against the sudden onslaught of brightness. As her eyes adjusted, the creaking sound began again. It seemed to be coming from behind her. Spinning around, Emily realized she had overlooked the second door next to the entrance to the room. She had checked the alcove, bathroom, and linen closet, but in the gloom, she hadn't seen the second door as she hurried to reach the stairs in the intermittent flashes of lightning.

She turned the lock in the doorknob and gave it a yank, but the door didn't budge. The creaking sound was louder now, but no voice answered her repeated calls. Running her fingers over the door, Emily tried to see what was preventing it from opening. Finding nothing, she got down on the floor to try and peer under it. A small, wedge-shaped rubber door stop was firmly shoved between the bottom of the door and the floor. Emily used the heel of her boot to kick at the stop until it finally slid back into the closet. This time when she turned the doorknob, the door opened easily at her pulling.

Emily fumbled for the light switch. The closet was in complete and utter darkness. She could now hear a whimpering sound coming from the back of the closet. Her fingers tripped over the switch. With one flick, light flooded the closet, and Emily fell to her knees beside the figure rocking rapidly back and forth, the floor creaking beneath her. Dragging as gently as she could with shaking fingers and her cumbersome cast, Emily removed the gag from Helen's mouth. The second she dropped the offending rag, she pelted Helen with questions, but the woman only continued to whimper, her eyes disoriented and unfocused. Emily made quick work of removing the bonds from Helen's ankles and wrists, but Helen was too weak to stand. Emily was concerned by the pallor of her friend's face. Her cheekbones jutted and her eyes were glassy. Helen was a small woman by nature, sporting a trim, athletic build, but now she looked positively emaciated. Emily chafed at Helen's wrists, murmuring reassurances to her. When Helen began to cry in earnest, Emily rocked her like a baby, her own vision blurred with tears. Jim had been killed the previous Thursday. Today was Wednesday. Helen had, in all likelihood, been locked in this closet for the entire ensuing week. How could Arlene have done this? Helen was her friend. But then again, a woman who could kidnap a child and then commit murder in order to keep him would surely have no qualms about holding someone hostage, even if it was one of her friends.

Though she hated to leave Helen even for a minute, Emily took the time to race to the kitchen and snatch the orange juice she had seen earlier in the fridge. Once she managed to get some down Helen, she seemed to rouse a little. In a voice hoarse from disuse, Helen told Emily, in halting fits and starts, that she was sure Arlene had been drugging her through her food. When Arlene had last come to check on her, Helen had refused to eat. Arlene had shoved some water at her, telling her she had better drink up while she could because this would probably be her last chance. She then told Helen that she had a foolproof plan to pin Jim's murder on her. She was upset, though, because now she needed to hurry things up. She had spotted Stephen in town.

Afraid of becoming dehydrated, Helen had drunk the water. It wasn't until Arlene had left her again that Helen realized the water had been drugged too. She suspected that whatever she'd been giving her, Arlene had put in a much larger dose this time.

Helen's voice began to slur again, and she was having trouble focusing on Emily's face. Her eyelids drooped, but Emily couldn't let her lose consciousness now. She had to get Helen out of there before Arlene came back. Helen weighed practically nothing, but with only one good arm, there was no way Emily could carry her all the way to the car. She hated to take the chance of waiting on Tad, as it seemed increasingly doubtful he had gotten her message, but she didn't see what other choice they had. Surely Detective Gangly-Arms would get the message she had left for him. Emily tried to haul Helen to her feet, but she was dead weight. Emily smacked her cheeks lightly and gave her some more orange juice. Emily tried to keep her conscious by keeping up a running monologue. She told Helen that they'd all been looking for her, that everyone knew she was not guilty of murdering Jim, that Duke was safe at Emily's parents' house, and that she and Gabby had been to visit her mother at Serenity Falls. The mention of Duke and her mother seemed to penetrate the haze in Helen's brain. Her eyes, although still cloudy, focused on Emily's face.

Emily gave her an encouraging smile. "There you go. You're strong. We're going to get out of this. I promise. Tad is on his way." Or, at least, she hoped he was. Helen nodded as if she understood, so Emily continued. "You mentioned a Stephen. Did you mean Stephen Olsen? Did you know that Jim was his brother? Had you and Jim both figured out that Stevie is actually Stephen Olsen's missing son?"

Again, Helen nodded. She was attempting to speak, when her eyes shifted. They filled with terror. Emily twisted around to see what had frightened Helen. Arlene stood in the closet doorway, the Glock in her hand pointed directly at them. Emily had been too busy trying to revive Helen to listen for Arlene.

Arlene's voice was pleasant, but her eyes flashed with malice. "You're mistaken, Ms. Taylor, just as Jim Layton and my friend Helen here were. Stevie is *my* son. I raised him. I took care of him. I saw to it that he had everything he could ever need or want. *I* am his mother." Her voice rose, but the gun never wavered. "Do you hear me? Stevie is *my* son!"

CHAPTER SEVENTEEN

———

Despite finding Jim's body and being run off the road, Emily realized that she had never known true, stark terror until that moment. She was literally staring madness in the face. She didn't know how she hadn't noticed it before, but it was obvious now. Shifting to keep Helen behind her, Emily tried to stand up. Arlene ordered her back to the floor. Emily slumped back down, knowing full well that Arlene wouldn't hesitate to shoot her on the spot. Desperate to buy some time, Emily asked, "Where's Stevie? Is he okay? Does he know what you've done?"

"What I've done?" Arlene looked incredulous. "What I've done is provide a loving home with a devoted mom for a child who deserved it and was denied the chance."

Emily could see the fire of conviction in Arlene's eyes, and another thought occurred to her. "You loved Stephen Olsen, didn't you? But you thought he and his wife didn't deserve their baby because she was suffering from postpartum depression, unable to care for their son."

Arlene waved the gun in the air, and Emily backed up a little further. "Postpartum depression?" Her voice was high and thin. "That woman just didn't want to be bothered by a baby. It interfered with her shopping and sleeping." Her lips tightened. "'It.' That woman actually called him 'it.'"

Emily nodded, hoping she looked sympathetic rather than terrified. "I can see why you would find that so horrible. Stevie is a wonderful boy."

The gun lowered slightly, and Arlene smiled in a way that made Helen whimper behind Emily. "He is exactly like his father. Kind, smart, beautiful. That's why I named him Stevie. He never looked like a Jacob anyway. I did love Stephen, but he spent all his time doting on his wife. He hired me so that I could be the one to take care of that baby. He never even saw me."

"That must have hurt your feelings," Emily said, trying to keep Arlene talking.

"Hurt? Guess so, but I was used to it. My mom was too busy trying to climb the corporate ladder to ever bother with me. But my dad, my dad was wonderful. Why couldn't Stephen have been more like my dad?"

"I don't know," Emily said. "What's your father like?" And where was he, she wondered. Surely a father, if he was in his right mind, would never let his daughter get away with kidnapping a child.

"My dad was taken from me when I was only seventeen. The hospital intern who fell asleep at the wheel and hit him head-on was probably a mother, too. An overworked mother, more concerned about her career than her baby. I was left with nothing and no one."

Emily wasn't sure what to say next, besides the truthful, "I'm so sorry for your loss."

Arlene stared into space for a minute, and Emily took the opportunity to try and stand up again. Arlene jerked the gun back in her direction, and Emily once again eased back down. "You have no idea what loss is. You have the perfect parents, friends like that Gabby with her beautiful children that she probably ignores, and Ted or Tad or whatever his name is who wants to marry you and have a family." Arlene shook with rage.

"Gabby is an excellent mother, and Tad is just my friend. Besides, I'm not sure I even want to have children. I worry I wouldn't be a good-enough mother. Not selfless enough. The way you are with Stevie."

Emily had hoped these words would soothe Arlene, but they only served to inflame her further. "Not sure you even want to have children? Must be nice to have that choice."

Emily stayed silent this time. Letting out a choked sob, Arlene said, "I had to have a hysterectomy when I was seventeen for severe endometriosis. I lost my dad the same day I had the surgery." Tears spilled over and left track marks down her flushed face. Emily's heart broke for the seventeen-year-old girl who had truly lost her whole world. But the woman Arlene had become had to be stopped. Her losses had snapped something in her, causing her to lose touch with reality. When Arlene swiped at the tears and steadied the gun with both hands, Emily knew their time was running out. Helen was gripping the back of her shirt so tightly she couldn't have moved if she wanted to. Since the sympathetic approach hadn't worked, she decided to try the defensive one. It probably wouldn't penetrate through Arlene's psychosis, but if she could keep her talking, maybe there would be time for Tad or Detective Gangly-Arms to show up. She didn't believe in ESP, but she still sent out fervent messages to Tad through the ether, begging him to hurry, to know what a desperate situation she was in.

Emily made her voice sound stern. "Arlene, you tried to kill Gabby and me once by running us off the road, but you didn't succeed. How do you think you're going to cover your tracks now? Helen's Tahoe is in your shed. Stephen is here in town. He won't rest now that he's found his son. You have nowhere to run this time."

"I told you before, Stevie is *my* son!" Arlene took a deep breath. The eerie smile was back. "You see, I didn't want to have to hurt anyone. Helen had been acting funny on our last run together, so I decided to follow her. I heard her making that appointment with Jim. I made sure to get there first. I didn't plan to kill him, but I had to make him see reason. The big oaf thought he could overpower me and drag me to the police, but I'm stronger than I look. We struggled, and I managed to get him with my pepper spray. I hit him in the back of the head with a hammer I keep in my bag for driving real estate signs into the ground. When he was knocked unconscious, I couldn't pass up the opportunity to get rid of him once and for all. I waited for Helen and used the pepper spray on her too. From there it was easy to bring both her and her vehicle back here. I've been letting Stevie hang out with his new friends so much, he never suspected a thing."

"Why didn't you kill Helen then?" Emily asked. Helen's grip on the back of her shirt was now choking her.

Arlene actually looked sad for a moment. "Helen is the one person who has truly taken the time to get to know me. I've had to keep us moving a lot so Jim couldn't find us. I know it was hard on Stevie, but Jim always seemed to be too close for comfort. I had hoped that finally hiding in plain sight would do the trick. It's been just Stevie and I for so long. But now that he's older and wants to spend time with his own friends, it was nice to have someone to talk to. I didn't want to hurt Helen. I've laid a careful trail for the police to follow. They already believe Helen is the murderer. I had hoped to disappear and leave it at that, but with Stephen in town, I'm out of time. The plans have to change."

Arlene motioned with the gun for them to stand up. Emily had to help Helen to her feet, and the woman swayed against her, the drugs and terror making movement practically impossible. Arlene gave Helen an apologetic look, but the terrified woman never met her eyes. "I'm sorry, Helen. I really am. But I have to shoot you and Emily. The police will believe that you shot Emily for interfering and then killed yourself out of remorse. I need your bodies in your Tahoe, though, so that there will be no question that you were also behind the attempt on Gabby and Emily's life." She snarled at Emily. "You are the most infuriatingly nosy woman I have ever met. That brick I threw through your window never even slowed you down. The only reason I didn't just shoot you then was because you obviously cared about Stevie."

"Well, thank you very much," Emily said, surprised she could summon up sarcasm at such a moment. She got a gun jabbed in the ribs for her effort. Arlene marched them into the hall, Helen stumbling and Emily doing her best to keep them both upright with the use of only one arm. "You know, Arlene, the Tahoe is here. Won't the police find that suspicious?"

Arlene laughed. "I've already thought of that. Stevie and I are staying in a hotel an hour or so down the road. Once he's asleep, I'll come back and move the Tahoe to your duplex's carport. But for now, let's get you guys out there. We've had enough chitchat. It's time to get this show on the road."

Emily moved toward the back kitchen door at Arlene's prodding. "Open it," Arlene demanded. Emily stepped cautiously through the broken glass and pooling water. Cold air blasted through the broken windowpane. Emily's hand fumbled on the doorknob, which was now slick with moisture. "Hurry up!" Arlene snapped.

"Mom?" Stevie's voice from the hallway stopped Arlene in her tracks.

"Mom, is everything okay?" Stevie asked again, standing in the doorway, confusion written all over his face. "What are you doing? Ms. Taylor? Ms. Burning! Where have you been? People have been looking for you all week."

Arlene turned toward him, carefully hiding the gun behind her back. "Stevie, I need you to wait in the car. I *told you* to wait in the car."

"Yeah, I know, but you were taking so long, and I needed to use the bathroom. I thought Mr. Higginbotham was here to help you load the last boxes? His car's still out front. Where is he?"

Another voice from the hall spoke up. "Mr. Higginbotham is right here. You okay, Emily? Helen?"

Arlene knew she was trapped. She raised the gun, and Emily pounced. She and Arlene crashed into the cabinets as Emily slipped on the wet floor. Arlene's grip on the gun remained firm. Emily hung on to Arlene with her left hand, using her casted right arm as a club. Arlene grunted when Emily made contact, but she kept her hold on the gun. Emily dimly heard Tad yelling at Stevie to call the police, before he also grabbed Arlene, attempting to wrest the gun from her. In their struggles, the gun went off. The sudden boom in the small kitchen shocked everyone into silence. Then a high-pitched scream had everyone rushing into movement again. Tad had Arlene's arms pinned behind her. Stevie was sobbing into his phone to the 9-1-1 dispatcher, and Emily caught Helen as she fell, blood gushing from her arm.

"She's been shot!" Emily screamed hysterically. Immediately, a compress covered the wound, and Emily glanced around to see where it had come from. Mr. Barnes ordered Emily to keep constant pressure on it. She was too stunned by his presence in this bizarre nightmare to say anything, but she obeyed. She watched, everything dim and muffled as if she were underwater, as Barnes moved, one sleeve torn off his button-down shirt, to the sink. He tore off the other sleeve and held it under the stream of water. He returned to bathe Helen's face. "It's only a flesh wound," he assured them all. "But she's still losing a good amount of blood." He turned to Stevie and said calmly, "Is the ambulance on its way?" Stevie's Adam's apple bobbed as he nodded his head *yes*. Barnes's calm in the midst of all the chaos seemed to clear away some of the fog, and Emily finally found her voice. "What are you doing here?" she asked him.

"Apparently, Ms. Taylor, you're not only pesky, but also a thief." The words were delivered with his typical sneer. "After Mathletes' practice finished, Mr. Higginbotham discovered that his car had been apprehended."

"I figured you got tired of waiting and took the car on home. I did wonder why you hadn't left a note," Tad spoke up, shifting his weight ever so slightly to keep Arlene pinned to the floor. "Looks like you were too busy." His clenched jaw betrayed his fury at being left in the dark.

"As he had no other means of transportation, and I was still at the school," Barnes continued, "I offered him a lift. On the way, he got your message, so we rode to the rescue. Good thing that Cobra's fast."

Emily had to agree. "I think I may have a new appreciation for sports cars."

Barnes smiled a real smile at her, and Emily wondered if some kind of truce was in the making. His next words derailed that idea. "You sure do know how to make a mess of things." He motioned around the room, and Emily leaned back on her heels, surveying the wreckage. Tad was still holding on to Arlene, who was sobbing hysterically and trying to explain herself to Stevie. Emily wasn't sure if he was listening to her or not, though. He had one hand clenched in his fringe of hair, the other gripping his cell phone, occasionally responding to something the dispatcher said.

Sirens sounded in the distance. Arlene became even more frantic, pouring out assurances of how much she loved him to Stevie. They all watched as he slid down the wall to sit next to her. Tad released her enough to let her hold Stevie's hand. Emily checked to see where the gun had ended up, surprised to see it resting comfortably in Tad's hand. She gave him a raised-eyebrow look, but he just shrugged. Tad kept his eyes trained on Arlene as she furiously talked to Stevie in low, desperate tones.

Helen stirred, struggling to regain consciousness, just as Detective Gangly-Arms came storming into the kitchen, paramedics in tow. Emily stayed by Helen's side as she was loaded onto a stretcher, unsure of whether to ride to the hospital with her or stay to help Stevie. Barnes took the decision out of her hands. "I'll go with Helen. They'll need to take your statement." He motioned toward the detective. Emily hadn't thought he could surprise her any more than he already had, but then he tossed over his shoulder," Keys are in her. I'll pick her up at your place later." And then he disappeared out the door.

Emily turned to Detective Gangly-Arms. "We have to stop meeting like this," she joked, but he was not amused.

"We have two very different ideas of what 'butting out' looks like." He hesitated, then touching her lightly on the shoulder, added, "Thank you."

Emily spoke quietly, not wanting Stevie to overhear. "Helen's Tahoe is in the shed out back. Arlene is responsible for all of it."

The detective nodded. "We've been going over all of the old case files for the missing Olsen baby. A picture of the baby's nanny was put through a digital aging program. It's a clear match between Arlene Davis and the nanny, Bridget McMillan."

"What happens to Stevie now?" Emily asked him.

"We'll find his father, and hopefully, they can heal together. Stevie's going to have a long road ahead of him. Poor kid."

"Stephen Olsen is in Ellington," Emily reported. That was news to Gangly-Arms. He stepped away to bark some orders into his phone. This might have been the detective's first big case, but Emily thought he'd handled it well. She might even have to start calling him by his real name. Or not. She didn't want to get ahead of herself.

When the detective turned back to Arlene, by unspoken agreement, Emily and Tad flanked Stevie. "Arlene Davis, you are under arrest for the kidnapping and imprisonment of Helen Burning, the attempted murder of Emily Taylor and Gabriella Spencer, the kidnapping of Jacob Olsen, and the murder of Jim

Layton." The clink of the handcuffs made Emily wince at the sound of their finality.

Stevie stumbled and Tad caught him. "Why? Mom, why?" Emily felt her heart shatter as she witnessed the utter anguish on the boy's face.

"I did it for you, Stevie. You're my son. I love you. Never forget—I love you," Arlene kept calling back to him as a uniformed officer led her out to a waiting car.

Detective Gangly-Arms turned to Stevie. "I know you have a lot of questions. We'll get them all answered. But for now—" He didn't seem to know where to go with the statement. Stevie was not yet a legal adult, so he would have to be placed under someone's care until he could be reunited with his father.

"For now, he'll be staying with me," Tad told the detective, who nodded. "We'll bring him by the station later." Satisfied with the arrangement, Detective Gangly-Arms left.

The eyes Stevie turned on her looked so young and lost that Emily longed to gather him up in her arms like the little boy he seemed to be at that moment. "I don't understand," he whispered to her.

"I know, Stevie. I know. Mr. Higginbotham and I will try and answer all of your questions to the best of our ability."

"Will you tell me the truth?" he asked, his voice cracking on the last word.

"Yes." Emily brushed the hair off of his forehead and looked him directly in the eyes. "I promise." Then she opened her arms, and Stevie, caught between the stages of childhood and adulthood, stepped into them and sobbed like a baby into her shoulder. As she stroked his dark hair, her eyes met Tad's over Stevie's head. Tad nodded. Whatever it took, she knew they would be there for Stevie. They would make sure he made it through to the other side of this wasteland that his life had just become.

EPILOGUE

———

Five days later...

The three figures making their way up the front walk to the school moved slowly. Weariness and sorrow dogged their steps. The past few days had been some of the most difficult ones that each of them had ever had to face. The consequences of Arlene's actions were far reaching.

After her arrest, Arlene confessed to everything. She asked only that she be allowed to tell the whole story to Stevie herself. Emily and Tad had sat on either side of him while Arlene talked and sobbed, offering him their silent support. Emily marveled at the strength Stevie showed throughout the long ordeal. White as a sheet, and with his jaw firmly set, Stevie peppered this woman who had raised him with questions. Blow after blow rained down on him as he came to the realization that he was losing the only mother he had ever known, as she'd be going away for a very long time. He learned his biological mother had taken her life due to her grief at his loss. And now, the coach he had looked up to was mourned once again as a loving and devoted uncle.

Stevie's love for Arlene, the woman who had been his mother in name and deed for the past seventeen years, made every blow worse. When he stood to give his "mother" a hug before leaving, his eyes were dry and his terse "good-bye" angry. Over the next couple of days, he went from angry to confused, to devastated, to numb in swings and cycles. Emily and Tad did all they could to comfort him. They gave him space to vent and cry, and when he was ready, they took him to visit Helen, who was still in the hospital, recovering from shock, dehydration, and her gunshot wound. She told Stevie how excited Jim had been to find him. He had been closing in on Arlene's trail for years, but he never had expected that she would be the one to find him. Her ploy of hiding in plain sight backfired. Despite the years, Stevie looked too much like his father to escape his uncle's notice. Jim had taken one of Stevie's mouth guards after practice, without his knowledge, and had it tested. Once he was positive Stevie was his long-lost nephew, he called his brother. A file, containing solid proof of Stevie's identity, was mistakenly transferred from Jim's desk to Helen's by a student worker who mistook it for one of the test files she was supposed to deliver to the counseling office. Helen had gone to Jim and tried to hold him off. She was afraid of how Stevie would handle the news. She and Jim were meeting at the school, the night that he was killed, in order to come up with the best plan of action.

Stevie broke down at that point in Helen's narrative, but he thanked her for her concern and apologized for Arlene's actions. Helen had been quick to correct him there. Arlene, and Arlene alone, was responsible for what she had done.

The day after they visited Helen, Stephen Olsen came forward and asked to meet his son. The reunion took place at Tad's apartment. There were a lot of tears on both sides, but the father and son's connection was immediate. After talking into the wee hours of the morning, Stevie decided that he would return to New York with his "dad," a word he spoke hesitantly but had left Stephen Olsen grinning from ear to ear.

This morning, Emily had come to the school early with Tad and Stevie to watch Stevie say his good-byes. Stephen Olsen met them there to pick Stevie up. When it was Emily's turn to hug the teenager good-bye, she broke down. Stevie pushed his hair out of his eyes and looked directly into hers. "Ms. Taylor," he said softly, "one day you're going to make an amazing mom. You're already a terrific teacher." Emily continued to cry into Tad's shoulder as they waved the reunited father and son off. Tad's eyes were none too dry either by the time the two were out of sight.

Despite their exhaustion, Emily and Tad turned to their classrooms. Another assembly was scheduled for that morning. Principal Matthews lauded the bravery of Emily and Helen, who had been released from the hospital in time to be in attendance. Emily made her way to the podium and looked out at the sea of faces. Her voice shook as she said, "The true heroes are Coach Layton, who never gave up on his family, and Stevie, who has faced tremendous loss with great dignity. I say the Ellington High Eagles play hard for a winning season this year in order to honor these two brave men." Thunderous applause met her pronouncement.

* * *

Emily wasn't sure how, but she made it through the rest of the school day. All she wanted was to go home and not think for a while, but her classroom suddenly had a revolving door. Helen stopped by, her left arm in a sling a counterpart to Emily's casted right, to thank her for taking care of Duke, for believing in her, and for saving her life. More tears were shed. When Helen also thanked her for her kindness to her mother, Emily had to ask her about Mrs. Quinton's question about money. Helen excitedly explained that she had found a CD among her mother's papers that she had forgotten about in her addled mental state. Thankfully, the amount would go a long way toward helping with her mother's medical expenses. Before Helen left, she and Emily shared a laugh over Emily's dad's insistence on installing new security systems in both sides of their duplex. Although they both appreciated his efforts, it was his upgrade of their fire alarms that struck them as humorous. Emily's mom had been making her daughter and best friend nylon-rope lamps to celebrate their safety. Apparently, rope had become her newest creative outlet. While burning the ends of the rope to keep it from unraveling and installing the wiring for the lamps, Emily's mom had managed to set several small fires. Emily's dad had confiscated all of her lighters, but he still revamped all of their smoke detectors. Just in case.

Emily's next visitor, arriving right on the heels of Helen's departure, was Mr. Barnes. He stiffly expressed his pleasure that Emily had discovered Helen and stopped Arlene. Emily wondered if her now not-quite nemesis didn't have a little thing for their beloved counselor. Emily figured she better give Helen a heads-up, as another "just in case." When Barnes continued by saying he had a secret to tell her, Emily assumed his crush was about to be revealed. Instead, he shocked her temporarily speechless by admitting that he had a secret life as a romance writer. He said he knew Emily had suspected him at one point of being the one to murder Jim, which she promptly apologized for, feeling the heat sweep her cheeks. Barnes brushed it aside, however, and said he wanted to clear the air between them completely. Emily feigned complete surprise at his revelation and swore to keep his secret in gratitude for his helping to save hers and Helen's lives.

When Barnes finally left, Emily staggered to the teachers' lounge, desperate for a caffeine pick-me-up. Tad met her at the door with an ice-cold soda, and they slumped at the table, companionably reviewing the events of the last two weeks. They had spent an extended amount of time with each other lately, but their focus had been on Stevie. Now that he had returned to New York with his dad, Emily wondered where her and Tad's relationship stood. They never had discussed that kiss.

Tad asked, "What are your plans for this weekend? Besides resting up, of course." His tone was casual, his large hands turning his soda can around and around, leaving rings of condensation on the tabletop.

Emily winced. "I'll be trying to make it up to Gabby that she missed out on all the excitement. That's if you consider almost getting shot, excitement. And trust me, she does."

Tad laughed, a sound that spread warmth through Emily's belly. "Well, when you're done placating the wounded warrior, I was hoping you'd let me take you car shopping. And maybe out to dinner afterwards?"

He watched her closely as he waited for her to answer, so she tried not to let her excitement at the prospect of an actual date show too much. She put on a pouty frown. "You're going to have your work cut out for you. It won't be easy to replace that PT of mine. She's been my loyal companion for years."

Tad stood and stretched. With his trademark smirk, he said, "With your driving record, Pit, we'd probably better try and find a place that sells tanks." With that, he sauntered out the door.

This time, Emily didn't resist the urge—she stuck out her tongue at his retreating back.

ACKNOWLEDGEMENTS

I've always been the type of reader who scours every word of the acknowledgements page. I find it fascinating to see the amount of support and encouragement that surrounds authors, so I would be remiss if I did not thank those who have helped me accomplish this lifelong dream. First of all, I have to thank my mom for sharing her love of books and writing with me from an early age. She has always been my biggest cheerleader. I would be lost without you, Mom. Thank you to my dad for showing me I could accomplish any dream if I was willing to put in the time and effort and for teaching me to never quit, even when the going gets rough. I love you, Dad. Thank you to my outstandingly supportive and encouraging husband. Without you by me side, I don't know where our beautiful boys or I would be, though I suspect it would be still in our pajamas, watching a *Jessie* marathon. :) Thank you to my boys, the lights of my life, for telling people that your mom was going to be an author so that I had to live up to that title. You are the beat of my heart and the breath of my soul. And to my many students who also encouraged me to "practice what I preach" and work to make my dreams come true--every one of you will always hold a special place in my heart. To Gemma Halliday, thank you for giving your time and taking a chance on this fledgling author. I will forever be one of your biggest fans. Thank you to all of my professors at Pittsburg State University, especially Dr. Meats, Dr. DeGrave, Dr. McCallum, Dr. Morris, Dr. Carlson, and Lori Martin, for pushing me and inspiring me to believe in my writing. Thank you to Lori Norbury for your belief that this dream would come true. Here's to *Scary Cherry Tales*. And of course, thank you to my test readers. To Gabriel Franklin and Marilyn A. Entrikin, thank you for not only being two of the best friends anyone could ask for, but also for taking the time to give me thoughtful reviews on my manuscript. Gabe, you are world's best commuting buddy. And Marilyn, your photography skills are out of this world! Thank you for sharing your talent to try and make me look presentable. :) To Misty, Ellie, and Wyatt Ohnemus, thank you for being such amazing and dear cousins and for giving me honest feedback on Emily's first adventure. And to Connor Bobbett, thank you for reading this book and asking me insightful questions. Not many teenage guys would take time away from his summer break to help out an unknown author. You're one in a million! I hope I get to teach you one day. Finally, thank you to all of my family on both the Comstock and Coffman sides. I am truly the most blessed girl in the world. I thank God for each and every one of you.

ABOUT THE AUTHOR

Tracy D. Comstock is a small-town girl from Missouri. She lives in a home where she is outnumbered 3:1 by the males in her life: her husband and their two extremely adorable, but terrifyingly ornery sons. She has no pets as all living things, besides humans, of course, come to her house to die, including the victims in her books. All her life Tracy devoured books. Her parents' most effective punishment was grounding her from reading. Although she has a B.S. in Education and a Masters in Literature, she was nudged down the path to publication by encouraging (and sometimes threatening!) family, friends, professors, and students. When not working on Emily's adventures, Tracy is an adjunct instructor for several local colleges, where she gets to teach others about her greatest passion: writing.

To learn more about Tracy D. Comstock, visit her online at:
http://tcomstockmysteries.wix.com/tracycomstock

Enjoyed this book? Check out these other novels available in print now from Gemma Halliday Publishing:

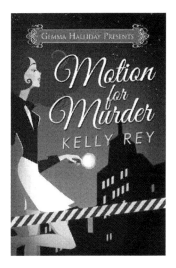

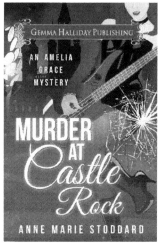

www.GemmaHallidayPublishing.com

5840275R00122

Printed in Germany
by Amazon Distribution
GmbH, Leipzig